DARKNESS RISES

AFTER THE EMP BOOK THREE

HARLEY TATE

ISBN: 9781521549780

DARKNESS RISES

A POST-APOCALYPTIC SURVIVAL THRILLER

A week after the unthinkable, would you still have hope?

With their house destroyed, the Sloane family sets off for the promise of safety in a cabin in Northern California. When a distress calls comes through on the radio, young Madison is adamant: a detour to the nearby college is the only choice.

What would you do to keep your family safe?

Walter hates to risk his family's life for the sake of a stranger. But his wife and co-pilot need antibiotics desperately and a college health center may be their best bet. Finding the strength to survive what happens next will be the hardest thing he's ever done.

The end of the world brings out the best and worst in all of us.

With the power grid destroyed and the government unable to help, the Sloanes are alone in a world losing hope. Will they survive a rescue mission or will the detour be the last stop on their journey?

The EMP is only the beginning.

Darkness Rises is book three in *After the EMP*, a post-apocalyptic thriller series following the Sloane family and their friends as they attempt to survive after a geomagnetic storm destroys the nation's power grid.

Subscribe to Harley's newsletter and receive an exclusive companion short story, *Darkness Falls*, absolutely free.
www.harleytate.com/subscribe

PROLOGUE

MADISON

Back Roads of Northern California
4:00 p.m.

"This is Mandy Patterson from Chico State. If anyone can hear me, we need help. Things are bad here. Real bad. There's five of us trapped in the radio building. We're almost out of food and water and we can't get out. The doors are locked from the outside."

Madison held her breath.

"We've tried breaking the glass, but it's got to be bulletproof or something. If we don't get out of here soon… we're all going to die. Please, if you're out there, again, this is Mandy Patterson from Chico State. I'm broadcasting from the radio building on campus."

The Sloane family listened to the girl over and over until she ended the broadcast. Madison swallowed. If they tried to save her, it would mean putting them all at risk again. But if they ignored it and drove on…

"We have to help her."

"Honey, we can't." Her mom turned around in the front seat. "We've already got seven people with us. There's nowhere for any more to go. You're crammed in the back seat with bottles of water, and Drew is up in the Jeep with three teenagers and enough boxed goods to make anyone claustrophobic."

"But she needs help!"

Her father spoke up. "We don't even know if it's real. How is she broadcasting? She can't do it without power. If they've got solar or wind or some backup generator, then she should be able to get out. I don't think it's worth the risk."

"Mom. Dad. Come on. What if that were me? What if I were stuck back at college begging for help? Wouldn't you want someone to save me?"

Her mom exhaled and closed her eyes. "Chico State has a hospital, right?"

Madison hesitated. "I don't know. It's smaller than a UC school, but it should have a student health center, at a minimum."

"That means current antibiotics for me and Drew."

"If there are any left." Madison's father glanced in the rearview. "This is a terrible idea. It's too risky."

Madison glanced out the window, trying to place their location. "We can't be that far from Chico. It's north of Sacramento."

Her father frowned. "I'd guess we're about thirty

miles due east." He glanced at her mom. "If we're going to make a detour, we should do it now."

Her mom turned in her seat. "You really want to do this?"

Madison nodded. "Yes."

"It will put all our lives at risk."

"I know."

"One of us might die. We could lose all that we have."

Madison knew the danger. But she couldn't leave someone to die. Not when she was pleading for help. "I know what we're risking, but we have to try. If we don't, what kind of people are we?"

Walter eased the car to the side of the road and honked the horn. The Jeep stopped just ahead. "Let's talk to the others. We'll put it up to a vote."

DAY SEVEN

CHAPTER ONE

MADISON

Back Roads of Northern California

5:00 p.m.

"You can't be serious." Brianna crossed her arms and leaned back against the door to the Jeep, her disdain written in the wrinkle between her brows.

"I know it's risky, but she could be just like us."

"*Pfft.* If she were just like us, she'd be a million miles away from college with enough supplies to see her through. Not crying for help on a radio asking for someone to do all the hard work to come save her."

Madison couldn't believe what she was hearing. Had a week without power and a few close calls already turned her friends and family cold? Were they already willing to ignore the suffering of others and only think of themselves?

If so, how different were they from animals? What separated them from the monsters of scary movies none of them would ever watch again?

Madison shook her head, flyaway strands from her ponytail brushing across her face. "At some point, we're going to need help. How can we ask for it if we turn a blind eye now?"

"So this is some karma trip? You want to go rescue some pathetic girl because if we don't it might come around to bite us in the ass?"

Madison's dad glanced up at Brianna, his scrunched brows hiding his brown eyes from view. Her father had already helped hundreds of people get to safety when he landed his commercial airliner on a private airfield. He'd made sure they had food and shelter and directions to the closest town before he set off on his own to find his family. And he'd taken his co-pilot Drew with him.

Her father was a good man. He could come around to her point of view.

"Dad, you have to agree with me. We can't leave her there."

He scrubbed at the week-old beard coating his jaw. "She said there were five, Madison. Five people trapped inside the building. Even if we get them out, what do we do with them? They can't come with us. There simply isn't enough room."

"So we just ignore them?"

"I didn't say that."

Madison thought back over the past week and of all the dangerous situations she had faced. First the causeway where they followed a semi-truck as the driver smashed his way out of a traffic jam with no end. Then the altercation with the police officer and the man who wanted to rob them. Those were the easy memories to relive.

The assault on her parents' house and the murder of her mother's co-worker Wanda were worse. So much worse. Those men wanted to kill them and steal their supplies. They didn't care who got hurt or who suffered.

Bill Donovan with his smug smile and protests of innocence. She ground her teeth together just thinking about the man. She'd had a chance to shoot him and make him pay for what he did to Wanda. But she couldn't do it with the whole neighborhood watching.

Children and families, still so clueless and unprepared. It had been a week since the power grid failed and still no word from the government. How long would they all stand around waiting for someone to help them? How long before they all realized this was as good as it was going to get?

Maybe shooting Bill would have woken them up. Jumpstarted their brains into survival mode instead of the cushy life they had all taken for granted.

It was too late to wonder.

Her parents' neighbors were miles away, tucked into their delusions and deteriorating neighborhood. But Madison could still help the people trapped in the radio building. She'd made a choice when she lowered the shotgun and walked away from Bill. The world as they knew it might be over, but Madison wouldn't turn into a monster. She wouldn't lose what made her human.

A bump against her leg caught her attention and

Madison smiled as she bent down to scoop up Fireball, the cat her mother saved from Wanda's apartment complex. She ran her fingers through his orange fur and the little guy purred against her chest.

"I know you all think I'm crazy and that going into that radio building will only put us in danger. But we can't turn our backs on everyone."

She glanced at her mother, who so far had stayed silent on the issue. "If you had driven by Wanda while she waited for the bus that wouldn't come, we would never have gotten to know her." Madison bent her head and snuggled Fireball closer. "We wouldn't have this little guy or her father's revolver or half of the food we managed to save."

Brianna shifted against the Jeep, her head bent as she stared at the asphalt beneath her feet. Her boyfriend Tucker spoke up from his position beside her. "Madison has a point. If Mr. Sloane hadn't helped Drew when he got shot, he wouldn't be alive. We've already made risky choices to help others. Why would we turn our back on people now?"

"Because it's a trap, that's why." Peyton ran a hand through his hair and took a step forward.

Madison glanced at him in alarm. He might have been the biggest man in the group, but Peyton had always been a softie at heart. "You're saying no?"

"We've been lucky so far, but at some point it's going to run out. Look at what happened to Wanda and Drew. They were shot for goodness' sake. We don't know what we're getting into going to Chico. The whole campus could be a war zone. We barely have any ammunition, and Drew and your mom are hurt. Your father has to be exhausted. None of us have slept more than a handful of hours in days."

He kicked at a dandelion struggling to grow in a pavement crack. "At some point we have to put ourselves first."

Madison turned to her mom. While they had debated, she hadn't said a word, her eyes focused on the burned skin of her left palm. Despite the expired antibiotics she had been taking, the blisters began weeping that afternoon, pus coating the angry red welts of raw skin.

"Mom, tell me you agree with me."

After a moment, her mom raised her head, pinning Madison with blue eyes that usually held so much kindness. Now all she saw in their depths was regret and sadness. "If it were just our family, Madison, I would say yes. But we're on the road to get Brianna home to her family's cabin in Truckee. Stopping to help strangers will only delay us more and put us in even greater danger."

Madison opened her mouth to argue, but her mother held up her injured hand. "At the same, we need medicine. Even if my hand heals, Drew needs antibiotics." She glanced over at the man who had accompanied Madison's father on his journey home. "Bullet wounds don't heal themselves."

Drew winced as he pushed himself up to stand, the sunken pallor of his cheeks reminding Madison of apocalypse movies she used to watch for fun. Part of her wished the end of the world had come with zombies. At least then they would all have a common enemy.

A bullet to the head wouldn't restore the power.

"I don't want you all to make a decision based on my needs." Drew ran his tongue over chapped lips. "There have to be a hundred pharmacies on the way to Truckee. We'll find one that hasn't been ransacked. We don't need to go to Chico. For all we know, it's already destroyed. A student infirmary has just as much reason to be broken into as a pharmacy."

Madison shook her head. "I don't agree. Townies don't go into college campuses. They don't even know about student health centers. If anywhere is going to have antibiotics, it's going to be there."

Her father cleared his throat. "We can talk about this until the morning, but it won't get us anywhere. I say we put it up to a vote. Majority wins." He glanced at Drew and then Tracy before focusing on his daughter. "I'm sorry, honey, but my vote is no. It's too risky."

Madison swallowed. From the way he stood so solemn and reserved throughout the debate, she had known her father would say no. But it still stung to hear him say it out loud. She turned to her mom. "What do you think?"

Her mom reached out with her good hand and gave her father's hand a squeeze. "I understand your reasons." She turned to Madison. "I vote yes on one condition: we go to the health center first. Antibiotics should be the priority. We need to save who we have before we think about saving anyone else."

Tucker spoke up next. "I vote yes, too. Even if it's a

trap, we should try. If we were stuck on campus, I would hope someone would have the decency to save us."

Madison smiled at Brianna's boyfriend. She had gotten to know him a bit through her roommate, but it had taken the end of the world for Madison to really bond with Tucker.

Brianna sighed next to him. "I vote no." She turned to Peyton. "How about you?"

Peyton glanced up at Madison. "Sorry, Madison. I vote no. Your dad is right. We can't risk it. After what happened to Wanda..." He trailed off and pinched the back of his neck, his face contorted with conflicting emotions.

Madison exhaled. "Obviously I vote yes, so that's three yes votes and three no votes." She turned to the only person left. "What do you say, Drew?"

He exhaled and glanced at her father. "I don't think it's right for me to make the call. Walter already risked his life to save me. I can't ask him to do it again." He rubbed at his wound. "I'm abstaining. You all will have to figure this one out."

Madison groaned to herself. *A tie? How could this be?* She stepped toward Peyton. "I know you're upset about Wanda, but can't you see we need to do this?"

"For all we know someone else is already there rescuing that Mandy chick and her friends."

"And if they aren't?"

"It's not our problem, Madison."

"But they'll die."

"She could be bait. We could be walking into something we can't get out of. I went along with it when you all insisted on going into that convenience store and I kept my mouth shut when your mom and Brianna and Tucker hit the Walmart. But I can't go along with this. One of these times, someone is going to die." He shook his head. "This time it could be you."

Madison blinked. Peyton voted no to keep her safe? She glanced at her father. He stared at Peyton with an expression Madison couldn't read. Were they in on it together? Had they talked about it somehow?

She shook her head. "You all are crazy. I can't believe you're just going to let this girl die." Madison stared at each person who voted no in turn. Her father, best friend, and roommate.

After a moment, Brianna pushed off the Jeep with a scowl. "Fine. I'll change my vote."

"Brianna, no!"

She waved Peyton off. "I'm only doing it because Madison's right. A student pharmacy is our best bet. And if that doesn't work, Chico State has a veterinary school. There will be antibiotics there."

"Are you sure?"

She nodded. "I looked into it when I applied to college. They have a huge agriculture department and vet program. It's not as big as UC Davis, but it's a close second."

Peyton glanced up. "If they have an agriculture department that means plants and seeds. Livestock, even."

Madison's father added his opinion. "There might be a truck we could use, too. We could swap out the Jetta for something that can transport more supplies."

He glanced at Brianna. “I hate the idea of showing up at your folks’ place empty-handed.”

“Then we’ll go? We’ll try to save those people?”

Her father exhaled. “Let’s find a place to make camp and sleep for the night. We’ll go first thing in the morning.”

DAY EIGHT

CHAPTER TWO

WALTER

California State University, Chico
8:00 a.m.

This is a terrible idea. He felt like Admiral Ackbar. The girl over the radio couldn't sound like more of a scam if she tried. His daughter's best friend pegged the whole scenario right from the start: sweet-sounding Mandy Patterson was bait.

He was heading into a trap with his injured wife, his former co-pilot with a bullet hole in his shoulder, and four kids who weren't old enough to drink. It wasn't that different from a grunt officer heading out on patrol.

Walter snorted. Reason one out of a hundred he opted for that flight contract. Flying in for a mission with no one to rely on but himself was easy. Placing his trust in a bunch of kids with guns they barely knew how to shoot was one of the hardest things he'd ever done.

These weren't seasoned Marines with a deployment or two under their belts. These were college kids who up until a week ago worried about exams and hangovers and whether their plants were growing all right. They hadn't seen combat. They didn't know what war was like.

Walter frowned at himself in the rearview mirror. His daughter shouldn't have to be a part of this. She should be tucked away somewhere safe while the world went to shit.

His wife should be relaxing and treating her burned hand. Instead she sat in the passenger seat with a pistol shoved under her waistband, checking for possible targets out the window.

Walter had made it home, but his family wasn't the same as when he'd left. He should be protecting them from the realities of this new existence and keeping them safe. Not leading them straight into danger and a potential trap they couldn't escape. He shifted the mirror to get a glimpse of Madison.

Only nineteen. So damn young and full of life. She shouldn't have bruises from a shotgun stock on her shoulder and cuts and scrapes from escaping a raging fire. She shouldn't have watched a woman bleed out from a gunshot wound or sifted through the wreckage of her home for things to salvage.

He'd failed her. A week into the apocalypse and Walter had failed to keep his family safe. But that would change. He tightened his grip on the steering wheel and turned his attention back to the road. From now on, no matter what danger they faced, he would ensure his family's safety.

Madison's roommate Brianna led the way in front of them with her canary-yellow Jeep. She claimed to know the way and despite wanting to be in front to scope out the situation, Walter had acquiesced and let her take over. As the Jeep slowed, Walter caught a glimpse of a sign up ahead.

California State University, Chico
Undergraduate Campus

He inhaled and glanced at his wife. "Looks like we're here."

Tracy nodded. He could tell by the lines around her mouth she was in serious pain, but she never admitted it. Her hand looked like rotting hamburger, raw and oozing. She needed better antibiotics. It was the main reason he'd given in at last.

Brianna pulled the Jeep over to the side of the road and stuck her hand out the window, waving them forward. Walter pulled up alongside and Tracy rolled down the window.

"I don't know where anything is on campus. It's been too long since I've been here. Do you want to take the lead?"

Walter leaned over his wife to answer. "Sure thing. First sign of trouble, I'll tap the brakes three times. Got it?"

Brianna nodded and the window rolled up.

Here we go. Walter eased past the Jeep and turned right onto campus. So far, the drive had been uneventful. When the road was clear, they were the only cars on it. When it was crowded with abandoned vehicles and accidents, it looked like a ghost town.

Every strip mall they drove by had been looted: windows smashed in, blackened soot clinging to the signs, debris littering the parking lots. A few places appeared intact, but Walter assumed it was by sheer force of will. Whoever sat inside those stores had serious protection.

He hoped the college would be spared from the chaos of the rest of town. As they drove down the main street, his daughter gasped in the back seat. *Guess hope didn't make it to Chico State.*

"Why would someone do this?" Madison's voice warbled as she stared out the window. "It's senseless."

Walter exhaled. The first building they drove by looked like a bomb had detonated inside. Papers littered the rangy grass out front, covering up the growing brown spots from lack of water. A soda machine sat on its side, front door pried open, dozens of cans sprawled in a circle around it. Someone had taken a spray can to the stucco, scrawling something about armageddon and justice.

"It doesn't take much to set off a mob." He'd seen it firsthand in LA twenty-five years ago. Then again in downtown Sacramento only a few days before. "Get enough people together and no law enforcement and this is what happens."

"But why?" Madison pointed out the window. "Why destroy things you can use?"

His wife spoke up next to him. "No one is thinking about the future. They aren't focused on what life will be like a year from now or even a month. Most people don't understand the gravity of the situation."

Madison mumbled something in the backseat before speaking up. "How long do you think before they figure it out?"

"That the power's never coming back on?" Walter mulled it over. "For some, the denial will last until their last breath. Others already suspect or know."

He wished he could save his daughter from all of this, but she needed to understand what they were up against and why sometimes she needed to say no and ignore cries for help. "There will be countless people who can't adapt. Without skills, and foresight, millions of people will simply starve to death over the next few weeks."

The next building they drove past looked the same as the first: broken windows and chaos. "Instead of breaking into stores for food, people broke in to steal TVs and sneakers. It's the same in any riot. People go for the things they think have value. No one places importance on food and water anymore. Those are too easy to come by."

"Not for everyone."

"In the major cities, it is. I saw it downtown. Grocery stores and pharmacies burned, all the stock turned to ash on the shelves."

Tracy agreed. "Those two guys in Walmart weren't

thinking about the future. They used half the ammo in that place for target practice."

Walter snorted in disgust. If he'd only been home, his wife and daughter would never have had to do the things they did. Their house would still be standing. All the supplies Tracy left behind in Walmart would be tucked away in their garage. He would never forgive himself for boarding that flight when his gut told him to go home.

"Dad, look! It's the cafeteria. They might have—" His daughter's excitement cut off mid-sentence as the building that once housed the campus dining hall came into view.

The red brick and yellow stucco still stood, marred by giant swaths of black soot and fire marks. Every window gaped at them, showing off the blackened maw of destruction inside the building.

"All that food. All the supplies. Gone." Madison's voice took on a tinny quality and Walter glanced in the rearview in time to catch her wipe at her cheek. "Where are all the students?"

"It was spring break, remember? The ones who stayed on campus are probably on the road by now. As soon as the campus police force broke down, the whole place probably devolved into a riot. Most kids wouldn't stick around to ride it out."

Tracy shifted in the passenger seat. "Let's find the student health center. Then we can talk about helping that girl."

"We are helping her, Mom."

Walter bit back a comment. Now wasn't the time to

take a side. "Keep your eyes out. As soon as you see a sign for the health center, let me know."

They drove through most of campus, circling down and back on every road in an attempt to find the place. There wasn't a single part of campus untouched. Every third or fourth school building had been struck by vandals and looters. Walter's hope dimmed with every new block.

"There! It's right over there!" Madison jabbed her index finger at the window and Walter followed the trajectory. A newer building sat at the end of the block, the outside apparently unharmed. "It looks all right!"

Walter pulled into the parking lot one building over and parked next to an abandoned vehicle. Brianna pulled in the Jeep beside them. Everyone piled out and stretched their legs.

"Do you think it's empty?"

"Without any windows busted out and no fire damage?" Walter shook his head. "Not a chance."

"That's what I was afraid of." Peyton frowned at the building. "Whoever's inside is doing a good job of keeping everyone out."

"It doesn't matter." Brianna pulled the rubber band out of her hair and redid her ponytail, collecting all the ringlets up into a sloppy bun on top of her head. She dropped her voice as she continued. "Drew is getting worse by minute. He's too pale and his head is hot. He won't last much longer without medicine."

Walter nodded. He'd feared as much. "Tracy needs medicine too."

"I'm fine."

He smiled at his wife. "I can tell you're in pain, dear. You put on a brave face, but that hand is killing you. You need pain medication and better antibiotics."

Walter surveyed the motley crew assembled around him. Drew hadn't even gotten out of the Jeep. He couldn't be counted on to do anything but keep breathing, if he managed that. That left two young men, himself, his injured wife, and Madison and her roommate.

He scrubbed at his face. Could any of these kids be trusted? Could he ask them to risk their lives to help his wife and co-pilot? Unfortunately, he didn't have a choice. "All right. Here's what we're going to do. Peyton and Tucker, you will come with me. The rest of you can wait here."

Brianna stomped her foot. "No way!"

"Dad, you're being ridiculous." Madison stared at him like he'd grown another eye.

Tracy leaned closer. "Can I talk to you for a minute? Alone?"

CHAPTER THREE

TRACY

California State University, Chico
1:00 p.m.

As soon as they were out of earshot, Tracy focused on her husband's face. She knew he wanted to protect her and their daughter, but asking both of them to stay on the sidelines would never work. She smiled. "I know you mean well, Walt, but you can't ask all the women to stay here."

"Of course I can. I just did."

Tracy laughed. "True. But it's never going to happen. Brianna is as tough as nails. She's from a full-on prepper family. She's been handling weapons since she could read and she's a hell of a lot more trustworthy in a firefight than her boyfriend Tucker."

Walter opened his mouth but closed it just as fast.

He exhaled and focused on the ground, rubbing the back of his neck as he thought it over. "What about Peyton? The kid's NFL linebacker size."

"But a complete teddy bear. He's coming around, but guns aren't his strong suit." Tracy paused. "If Madison were in danger though, the boy would walk through fire and not hesitate."

Walter nodded, almost wincing as he tried to ask a question. "Are they…?"

"No. Still friends as far as I know."

Her husband sagged in relief and Tracy couldn't help but chuckle. "Your daughter's nineteen, Walt. It's okay if she has a boyfriend."

"It'll never be okay, Tracy. But I'm trying."

"I know." Tracy reached out and squeezed his arm. "We're all tough. Every last one of us."

Walt's lips thinned. "I'm sorry I didn't come home that morning. I had a feeling something was wrong, but I had a job to do and—"

Tracy shushed him. "I don't blame you at all. You did what you thought was right. We all have. Heaping guilt on your shoulders will do nothing but weigh you down."

"From what it sounds like, you almost died at that Walmart. If I had been home, it would have been me on that run."

"We survived."

"Wanda didn't." Walter ground his fist into his palm.

Tracy knew her husband blamed himself for everything that happened to her and Madison over the last week. Somehow she needed to shake him loose of his worry and doubt. "No one could have predicted that night. Even if you had been there, the fire would still have been set. We would still have lost the house."

"I don't believe that."

Tracy exhaled. Arguing about the past would get them nowhere. She rose up on her toes and kissed her husband's cheek. "Let it go, hon. Focus on the here and now. Drew needs medicine."

"You do, too."

"Not as much as he does." She paused. Walter hadn't told her much about their trek through downtown, but based on the bullet hole in Drew's shoulder, it had to be terrible. "Will he be all right?"

Walter nodded. "With the right medication, yeah. He should recover." With one hand, Walter reached for her wrist and turned her palm up to face him. "Your burn looks bad, Tracy."

"I know. But I'm fine." She would never admit how much her hand hurt. At least the antibiotics she had been taking kept her sane and the pain had receded to a bearable level. She thought about the few hours after the fire, when she drifted in and out of consciousness and her daughter had to face the neighborhood alone.

Tracy shuddered. "We should come up with a plan of attack. Scope the place out and figure out the best way in."

Walter smiled. "You sound like a fire team leader."

Tracy glanced behind her at the four college kids huddled together. "I guess I am."

Her husband slipped his arm around her waist and brought her close enough to kiss. His lips brushed against hers. "When this is over and we make it to the cabin in Truckee, I'm taking you out into the woods and having my way with you."

A laugh bubbled up her throat and she couldn't keep it back. "Easy boy, you don't want to frighten the children."

After a quick kiss, Walter let her go. It was so good to have him back. One hug and the weight of the future lifted from her shoulders.

"Let's find a place to set up camp nearby and we can come up with a plan. I want to go in at dusk."

* * *

STUDENT HEALTH CENTER, CSU CHICO
6:00 p.m.

TRACY STARED AT THE BACK OF HER DAUGHTER'S head as she bent over the map Walter had drawn of the health center and the surrounding buildings. For every word she told her husband of her daughter's bravery and ability to fight, another word echoed inside Tracy's head.

Love.

She loved her daughter more than anything in this world and part of her wanted to wrap her up in bubble wrap and keep her safe from the reality they now faced. But she couldn't do that if an infection set in.

Tracy glanced down at her hand. The worst of the burn oozed a milky, yellowish fluid. She had tried wrapping it in bandages, but that only held the infection in. If her hand had any hope of healing, the wound needed to drain and she needed the strongest antibiotic she could find.

Drew fared even worse. That afternoon, he'd fallen asleep and been almost impossible to rouse. His wound was swollen and discolored, the duct tape barely visible beneath the puffy tissue.

She knew they had to stay behind, but the thought of sending her daughter out on this run twisted her insides. Madison and Brianna talked the plan over, pointing at the ground and hashing out who would do what while Walter talked Peyton through their maneuver.

Tucker leaned against the side of the Jeep beside Tracy and crossed his arms.

"Unhappy about being left behind?" she asked.

He kicked at the dirt. "No. Yes." He exhaled in frustration. "I don't know. I just don't like Brianna going back out there. After the Walmart, I just..."

Tracy nodded. Tucker had come up with a plan to rescue his girlfriend when the two idiots with more bullets than brains had started shooting up the bedding department. Thanks to his idea and Tracy's ridiculous acting, they all made it out alive. But this time, they might not be so lucky.

She smiled as he looked up. "She's tough as nails and Madison is with her. As long as they stick to the plan, everything will be fine."

"Brianna's not the best at following a script."

"Let's hope this time she can."

Tucker didn't say another word. Instead, he stood by Tracy's side. Both of them would be watching people they cared about leave on a mission they might not come back from. All to help Tracy and Drew. Tracy had been through countless goodbyes with her husband over the years: first deployments when he was on active duty, then two-week-long shifts as a commercial pilot.

Tucker probably only said goodbye at the end of a school term. She nudged him. "Do you love her?"

He glanced up at Tracy, face so young, but earnest. "More than anything. Brianna's all I have."

"Then go hug her and tell her that before she leaves. Maybe it'll help keep her focused."

Tucker nodded and pushed off the side of the 4x4. Tracy watched as he tapped Brianna on the shoulder and pulled her up for a hug. Brianna hugged him back with a fierce determination that spoke to her courage and strength.

Madison stood up and made her way over to Tracy. "We'll be fine, Mom. We'll get you better medicine, find some for Drew, and be back here before you know it."

With her good hand, Tracy reached out and Madison eased in for a hug. She remembered when Madison only came up to her waist and would wrap her little arms around her thigh so tight, squeezing like if she let go, Tracy might disappear.

The first day of kindergarten, Walter had to pry his daughter's arms apart and send her on her way. Today, Madison was already pulling back, eyes focused on the building, body itching to go. Tracy gave her daughter a last pat and watched with a trapped breath as she joined her father on the edge of the parking lot.

Tracy sent up a silent prayer. *Please keep them all alive. Please.*

One by one, Brianna, Madison, Walter, and Peyton disappeared from view.

CHAPTER FOUR

MADISON

Student Health Center, CSU Chico
6:30 p.m.

"The back entrance is right up those stairs." Brianna pulled down her binoculars and pointed at the building before handing them to Madison.

"What if it's locked?" Madison adjusted the focus and zeroed in on the back of the student health center. It was a newer building, made of concrete with stucco and brick veneers. A pair of double doors stood in the middle of the rear, flanked by narrow windows on either side.

"Double doors are easier to kick in than singles. Even if it's locked, we should be able to bust them open." Brianna paused. "Unless there's a metal support in the middle. Then we're screwed."

She motioned for the binoculars back. After looking

through them again she nodded. "We should be able to fit through one of those windows on the side. Assuming they're tempered, a good hit from a rock on the bottom corner should break one."

"That's it?"

Brianna nodded. "Tempered glass is safety glass. It's used for schools, hospitals, car windows. Anywhere sharp glass would be a hazard. It doesn't break the same way regular glass breaks. One good hit at a point of low flexion and it'll shatter into tiny, non-sharp pieces."

Madison exhaled. "Where did you learn that?"

Brianna shrugged. "My dad. He taught me how to break into most places just in case."

Madison shook her head. While her father had been playing goalie for every one of Madison's soccer kicks in the backyard, Brianna's dad had been teaching her how to survive when the world went to hell. It must have made for a difficult childhood for Brianna, but now Madison wished her father had shared a bit of the Clifton family crazy.

With a motion of her hand, Brianna took the lead, easing away from the building that gave them cover and into the open parking lot. Madison hurried to catch up. "My dad said to wait until he gave the signal."

"I know, I want to be ready. We can hold up in the nook beside the stairs. It's getting too dark to see anyone out here. I don't want to be caught in the parking lot before we ever make it inside."

Madison frowned. It wasn't how they had rehearsed it an hour before, but it was too late. "Fine. But no more deviations, okay?"

"Sometimes deviations are necessary."

"We have a plan for a reason."

Brianna made it to the stairs and crouched down beside them. Madison followed.

"Plans have to adapt and change. Sometimes the plan goes wrong and you need to make a judgment call to fix it."

Madison didn't know what to say. Brianna had stood beside her the entire time her father outlined the plan, nodding her head in agreement. Now it sounded like she wasn't going to play along one bit. "So you're saying to hell with it? You're just going to barge in there and ignore everything my dad said?"

"No. Not at all. I'm going to follow the plan as long as it's the right thing to do. But as soon as it isn't, I'm improvising."

Dusk had settled on campus, the trees across the parking lot barely visible to Madison's naked eyes. Even the building they had crouched behind only a minute before was more apparition than structure. In another few minutes, they wouldn't be able to see more than a few feet in front of them.

Maybe Brianna's idea had been the better one. She sighed. "How do you know what decision is right?"

"Whatever is the most expedient in the moment."

Madison shook her head. "It's not that simple."

Brianna scoffed. "Of course it is."

"You're telling me you'd shoot someone if it was the fastest way to get what you needed?"

"If shooting someone kept me alive and got me something I needed, then yes. All that matters now is staying alive. Everything else—morality, ethics, a sense of justice—it's noise."

Madison couldn't believe her ears. Was the dark somehow clouding Brianna's perception or did it give her the freedom to say what she had felt all along? She thought back to the causeway and how Brianna gunned the Jeep to ride the wake of the semi-truck while it barreled down car after car. How she didn't bat an eye when they walked into the convenience store and stumbled upon two dead bodies.

Was her former college roommate this cold? This devoid of humanity and compassion?

Madison swallowed. "What about me? Would you kill me if it was the most expedient choice?"

Brianna stayed silent for a moment. "Would you ever stand in the way of my survival?"

"Of course not."

"Then, no. But anyone who gets in my way is fair game."

On some level, Madison always knew Brianna had a backbone of steel. But hearing her talk about human life like it was a piece of rubble to step over, a temporary impediment to her path… She closed her eyes and the face of Bill Donovan filled her brain.

"Would you have killed Bill?"

"Before he got Wanda killed or after?"

Madison's stomach roiled. "Take your pick."

"Before, no. Your mom did a good job threatening the guy. But after? In a heartbeat."

"Then why didn't you? You were armed. When we

were standing there on the street, you could have taken the shot."

Brianna shifted in the dark beside Madison. "It wasn't my house that burned, Madison. Wanda wasn't my friend. I was sad that she died, but I barely knew the woman. I wasn't going to step into a fight that wasn't mine. I figured you would do what was necessary."

"But you don't think I did."

"Not that time, no."

Madison fell silent. The fact that she didn't pull the trigger when she had Bill in her sights haunted her. But he wasn't armed and she didn't know for sure that he had been the one to set fire to the house. What if the man they had captured was lying? For all they knew, he was using Bill as a scapegoat to cover up for the real perpetrator.

She couldn't kill a man when she didn't know if he deserved it. Not then… maybe not ever. Did that make her weak? Was this new world reserved for those who could turn off their sense of justice when the situation called for it?

"What about Tucker? He voted to come here and help the girl in the radio station. He found a way to escape Walmart without killing anyone."

Brianna mumbled under her breath.

"What did you say?"

"I said, he's a sweetheart."

"So he's exempt from your necessity-begets-violence stance?"

Brianna's voice dropped again. "I didn't say that."

"Then what are you saying?"

It took so long for Brianna to respond, Madison began to wonder whether she would.

"He's not cut out for this life." Brianna stood up and leaned back against the wall. Her voice filtered down to Madison like a whisper from a ghost. "I'm not going to be able to protect him forever."

"You can't—" The sound of a bird chirping three times cut Madison's response short. "That's the signal."

Brianna hopped the rail and landed on the steps outside the double doors. "Let's do this." She reached for the handle, but it didn't budge. "Locked."

Madison pulled the multitool she had purchased at the sporting goods store from her pocket and handed it to Brianna. Her former roommate popped out a small knife blade and worked the lock, shimmying the blade back and forth, but it wouldn't budge.

She stood up. "Do you have any bobby pins?"

Madison shook her head. "No. What good would they do?"

"I need a tension wrench, something I can hold down to release the lock on top." Brianna patted her pockets searching for anything that might work when the distinctive pop of gunfire sounded from inside the building.

Brianna's eyes went wide and she spun to face the parking lot. "Find a rock! We're going in. Now."

CHAPTER FIVE

WALTER

STUDENT HEALTH CENTER, CSU CHICO
6:30 p.m.

NIGHT RAIDS ARE THE WORST. WALTER WOULD HAVE traded an air strike any day for entering a hostile situation on the ground with no support other than a handful of green kids with no combat experience.

From the cockpit of an F/A-18, he could acquire his target, launch his strike, and be out and away before anyone could even fire a shot. Anonymous and lethal, just the way he liked it.

This was neither. Ground combat with crap for weapons, only enough ammunition to play Russian roulette, and no visuals on the potential hostiles inside combined to make this mission incredibly stupid. And yet there he was, crouched in front of a metal door with a kid who outweighed him by fifty pounds standing around with his thumb up his rear end.

Walter exhaled. If his wife and Drew didn't need this medicine so badly, he would have taken his time to prepare. Gone in for reconnaissance a few times before busting the door down and making a scene. But Tracy assured him Drew needed antibiotics yesterday.

One look at the puss oozing from the man's swollen wound and Walter agreed. If they didn't pump Drew full of antibiotics soon, they would lose him. Walter wasn't going to let that happen. Not after he dragged that man's sorry ass through the tail end of a riot, broke the news about his dead fiancée, and got them both out of the city before the barricades shut them in.

He pushed down on the bent paperclip and shoved the unfolded one into the remaining space inside the lock. With his one hand maintaining downward pressure, Walter raked the straightened paperclip toward him, attempting to lift the pins inside the lock and unlock the front door.

Leave it to the student health center to cheap out on their hardware. A simple lock like this was easy to pick, even if it took a few tries. After raking his hand several more times, he heard a pin move. *That's it.* A handful more attempts and another two lifted. He tried the handle. It turned.

"How did you do that?"

Peyton's hushed question made him smile. "Practice."

He wished he could be doing this mission alone. To

risk his daughter and her friends for the sake of his wife and a man none of them knew too well didn't seem fair. But he couldn't keep Madison away, and her friends would be an asset whether Walter wanted to admit it or not.

With a deep breath, Walter leaned back and let out a cardinal's call—three small chirps, a pause, then another three. Hopefully Madison and Brianna were ready. He turned to Peyton as he stood. "Stay close."

Walter pulled a pistol from his waistband before swinging the door open. As it shut behind them, Walter clicked on his flashlight. He would have loved a little tactical version—something made of cast aluminum with rugged notches for grip and an adjustable beam. But the cheap trunk flashlight he scavenged from the rental car would have to do. Between that and the paper clips, that car was coming in handy.

With a flick on and off of the flashlight, Walter assessed the situation, handgun light and easy in his shooting hand. They stood in a waiting area about the size of Walter's living room before it turned to ash.

Nothing looked disturbed. Either they were incredibly lucky and the health center hadn't been looted or whoever was hiding out had been neat and tidy.

A hallway beyond led deeper into the building and an elevator off to the right at one time gave access to the upper floors. Now it just sat frozen in place like a Lego brick for a giant.

Peyton clicked on his flashlight—a slim little thing sold by the checkouts at sporting goods stores. It wasn't bad for a dollar. With an LED bulb, it might outlast them all.

Walter reached out and turned it off.

"Only use it when you have to. Quick bursts of light on and off. If there's someone else in here, your flashlight will tell them exactly where you are. It's easier to stay hidden in the dark." He let the flashlight go. "Think firefly, not floodlight."

Peyton shifted beside him. "Got it."

"Good." Walter motioned toward the wall. "Check the directory. See if you can find the pharmacy. I'm going to scope out the reception area."

Peyton headed for the far wall and Walter turned toward reception. The desk sat empty, a coffee mug abandoned on the top along with a stack of papers and a cup full of pens.

He leaned against the wall and used three bursts of light in different areas to scope inside the space. *Empty*. Walter hopped the desk and landed in a crouch. With his gun in his right hand and flashlight in his left, Walter crossed his arms at the wrists and crept forward.

There were so many places to hide. So many dead areas. He pulsed the light again.

Walter hadn't trained in ground combat or urban warfare since before Madison was born. Sure, he could shoot a handgun and a rifle and kept in shape, but he was no seasoned infantry Marine. He forced a breath into his lungs.

All that mattered was keeping his daughter and his wife safe and finding antibiotics. He shoved his momentary doubt aside. His family came first. He would walk through hell and back out again if it meant they could survive.

He flicked the light and climbed back over the desk. Peyton stood by the directory, not moving in the darkness. "Did you find it?"

"Suite 108. I'm assuming that's somewhere here on the first floor."

Walter nodded. "Stay behind me. We'll have to clear the hall and any rooms as we approach. If a gunfight starts, take cover anywhere you can."

"I can shoot. I'm not great at it, but I can shoot."

"I'd rather keep you alive. If I'm worried about where you are, I won't be as effective. Got it?"

Peyton grumbled his acceptance and Walter pressed forward. They needed to get on with it. With Madison and Brianna sneaking in the back, Walter had to clear the first floor and find the pharmacy as soon as possible.

He headed toward the hallway. Without any light from outside, the building was pitch black. No amount of adjusting to the darkness would give his eyes enough light to see. He turned on the flashlight and swept the hall.

Nothing.

Maybe they really were lucky.

Approaching the first door, Walter reached for the handle.

CHAPTER SIX

TRACY

PARKING LOT, CSU CHICO
7:00 p.m.

SITTING AROUND WAITING FOR HER HUSBAND, daughter, and two more college kids to return from a drug run wasn't how Tracy envisioned a single night of her life unfolding. But there she was, stuck with an injured hand and no way to help. She snorted her frustration out her nose and spun around.

"Enough waiting. We need a camp."

Tucker glanced up from his spot on the trunk of the Jetta. "What do you mean?"

"A place to stay and regroup for a day or two. If everyone makes it out of the student health center alive and they get medicine, Drew needs to take it and rest. We can't go anywhere until he's a bit more stable."

Tucker turned and peered into the back of the Jetta. "Do you think antibiotics will even work?"

Tracy wished she knew. "All we can do is hope. But in the meantime, we can make him more comfortable and give us all a place to rest. If we stay up in shifts, at least we can all get a few hours of sleep later."

"Makes sense." Tucker pointed up the road. In the growing dark, they couldn't see anything beyond the buildings at the edge of the parking lot. "Houses start about a block that way. When we drove by, they didn't look all that bad. I bet we can find one to use for a while."

"Good. I'll check on Drew and secure the Jetta. You put anything away that came from the Jeep and lock it up. We can check out the houses together."

Tracy walked over to the rear seat where Drew rested and bent down to feel his pulse. His heart still pumped, but his breath came even more shallow than the last time she had checked. Even if they did get him medicine, it might be too late. Tracy pushed up to stand and eased the door shut.

As long as Drew stayed still, no one would notice him from the road. They couldn't keep an enterprising thief from breaking into the cars, but hopefully they wouldn't be gone for long.

Tracy locked the doors to the Jetta and pocketed the keys as Tucker did the same with the Jeep. As they met between the vehicles, she handed him a flashlight. "Only use it if you have to. I'm hoping we can get all the way to the houses without them."

"What about weapons?"

"I'll bring a handgun. As long as we stay together, we should be fine."

Tucker's head bobbed up and down, his black hair blending into the dark as he turned toward the street. "Let's see what we can find."

Tracy led the way, keeping close to the shadows and as concealed as possible. Just as Tucker promised, after they cleared the block, the school buildings gave way to little houses tucked close to the sidewalk, front porches barely visible in the night.

Motioning for Tucker to stop, Tracy pointed up at the first house. "Do you remember which ones were still intact?"

"Most of them, actually. I only saw one or two that had any kind of damage."

"All right." Tracy made her way farther down the sidewalk, passing the first two houses with her gun held loose, but firm in her good hand. "We'll pick the farthest one off the street on this block."

Six houses. All appeared fine, like the owners were nestled away safely inside, without a care in the world. Tracy didn't know if they were occupied, vacant, or harboring people just like themselves. But they needed a place to sleep.

She backtracked, stopping in front of a pale house with dark shutters. "Let's try this one. "It's got good cover from the trees for the second story windows."

Tucker nodded and the pair approached the front porch. Tracy touched Tucker on the arm. "Wait at the foot of the stairs. Let me check it out first while you watch the street."

He did as she instructed and Tracy climbed up to the front porch. A swing hung from the porch ceiling to her right and a dead potted plant greeted her beside the front door. If anyone was still home, they'd given up on the flowers a few days before.

She reached for the door handle. It turned. Was that a good thing or not? Tracy didn't know. She pushed the door open and waited, wishing she had training for this sort of thing. Breaking into houses wasn't in a librarian's skill set.

"It's unlocked. I'm going in." Tracy didn't wait for Tucker to respond. Instead, she ducked inside and braced herself. If anyone wanted to shoot her, now would be the best time. She couldn't see more than a foot in front of her.

After counting to two hundred, she stuck her head back out the front door. "Come on in."

Tucker appeared by her side a moment later. "Is it clear?"

"I have no idea." Tracy shut the door behind him and flicked on a small flashlight. "But I can't see anything, so we'll have to use this."

Tucker clicked on his own. "Let's split up." He moved the beam around the house, lighting up a small entry, an empty living room, and stairs leading up to the second floor. "I'll take the upstairs."

Tracy nodded. "I'll start on this floor. We can meet back here."

"I'll shout if there's a problem."

Tracy watched Tucker climb the stairs and disappear down the hall before heading off on her own.

Making her way through the open living and dining rooms and into a small, but tidy kitchen, she grew more relieved every minute. From the lack of upset, it appeared whoever lived there had packed and left when the power went out or hadn't been home at the time.

The house was full of nice furniture, old but well-maintained. It struck her as a professor's place, but they were in the middle of spring semester, so it didn't make sense. A professor would be teaching, not on vacation.

Then it clicked: spring break. UC Davis had been on spring break. CSU Chico must have been as well. From the looks of the rest of campus, it appeared a good number of kids had stayed on campus, but it made sense for a professor to take a few days off.

She entered the back hall and found a tastefully furnished bedroom and half bath before walking into a home office.

With books lining the walls from the floor to the ceiling and a desk sitting in the middle, it had all the feel of scholarly learning combined with a sense of home Tracy would never have again.

A worn plaid blanket was draped over the arm of a wood captain's chair on wheels. Tracy ran her fingers across the wool.

Never again would she relax with a cup of coffee and stare out her kitchen window at the flowers spilling over the pots in her backyard.

Never again would she sit with Walter on the couch and watch a ball game, waving at the occasional neighbor who walked by.

She eased down into the chair and spun to face the

desk. Picture frames dotted the top, full of smiling faces of a man and a woman. In one, they stood in front of a scenic tropical backdrop, grinning as they held up hands with matching wedding bands. In another they waved from atop a small mountain, nothing but blue sky in the distance.

Treasured memories of the everyday world. The one they had all taken for granted. The one that ceased to exist in the blink of an eye. No more baby clothes or handmade Christmas stockings. No more flipping through yearbooks or photo albums.

Everything Tracy had held onto for Madison's entire life, gone up in smoke. Turned to ash.

Maybe it was for the best. Losing everything made leaving that much easier. She knew they would have to do it eventually. But it still hurt. She wiped at her eyes with her good hand and stood up. Memories would have to suffice.

Tracy couldn't dwell on the past. Every second she delayed was a second she put her family at risk. She took a step when a sticky note on top of the desk caught her eye.

SMF to LGA, Saturday 8:10 a.m.

Hotel Indigo Lower East Side, 4 p.m. check-in

LGA to SMF, Thursday 10:17 p.m.

If the note described the travel plans of the husband and wife who called this house a home, the chances of them ever making it back were slim. Flights weren't leaving LaGuardia or landing in Sacramento any time soon.

Tracy took one last look around and strode out of the room to find Tucker waiting by the front door.

"It's all clear upstairs. I think whoever lives here left on vacation."

"I agree. Let's check out the back and then we can move the cars over."

Tucker nodded. "There's a detached garage at the end of the lot. We might be able to stash at least one back there."

After confirming the garage and the backyard held nothing but tidy tools and withered tomatoes, Tracy and Tucker moved the two vehicles and unloaded as much as feasible with only two sets of arms and one damaged hand. After securing the cars, they hauled a practically unconscious Drew into the house.

As Tucker propped the man's legs up on the living room sofa, Tracy stood up and stretched. "Now that Drew's safe, one of us should go back and wait." She shined her flashlight on her analog watch. "They should be back any time."

"I'll do it. You can relax and keep an eye on Drew."

Part of Tracy didn't want to expose Tucker to any more risk. He'd been through so much already. They all had. "Are you sure?"

"Yep. You rest. I'll head back."

Tracy nodded and watched in silence as Tucker

grabbed a bottle of water and pocketed his flashlight. He eased out the front door and stood on the step, letting his eyes adjust to the dark, before heading back toward the student health center.

Once he disappeared from view, Tracy locked the front door and sat on the upholstered bench in the front window. Her hand throbbed from too much exertion and the occasional bump of the wound. She hated not being fully capable.

Staring out into the dark of the university town, Tracy tried to keep the internal demons at bay. Her husband and daughter were out there, searching for medicine because of her. If something happened to one of them, she didn't know if she could forgive herself.

So many things had happened in such a short time. If this was only the beginning, what lay ahead? How much harder would it get? How many of them would make it?

After pulling the handgun from her waistband, Tracy checked to make sure it was loaded and ready and set it in her lap. All she could do was wait and pray.

CHAPTER SEVEN

WALTER

STUDENT HEALTH CENTER, CSU CHICO
7:30 p.m.

THE SECOND THE HANDLE TURNED, WALTER KNEW they weren't alone. It could have been a shuffling noise or a whisper from the other side or just the hair on the back of his neck, but he knew.

As the door swung open, Walter pulsed his flashlight beam. Nothing obvious.

Damn it.

His heart thudded like a freight train chugging up a mountainside. *In or out. In or out.*

There wasn't a good option. Too little light, not enough men. He glanced at Peyton. Not enough experience.

If they could clear the room… The crack of

something wooden connecting with Peyton's head shocked Walter out of his hesitation. He spun, gun up, flashlight on.

A man stood in the hallway holding a block of wood like a baseball bat. A two by four, Walter guessed. With the light in the man's eyes, he couldn't see, but he could still swing. The wood flew in Walter's direction. Even in the chaos, he could see the blood. Peyton's blood.

All because Walter didn't know what to do. Peyton sagged to the floor next to him, lifeless and awkward.

Was he dead? Unconscious? Bleeding out? Walter didn't know and didn't have time to wonder.

The man swung the weapon again, blind and full of fear and rage. He grunted as it whipped an inch in front of Walter's face.

Walter couldn't leave Peyton. The kid took up half the doorway, pushing the door open wide with his body.

The smart thing would be to retreat, get in a corner, somewhere, anywhere to protect Walter's rear. But he couldn't leave Madison's best friend. If he died on Walter's watch…

He had to act. Enough hesitating. Enough trying to do the right thing. His daughter was either inside or on the other side of the back door and Walter wasn't going to let her be hurt or killed.

Worse.

The trigger pulled so easy. The gun had been used often, broken in until the pull was smoother than a hot knife through butter. The noise of the single shot pierced the silence.

The two by four clattered to the ground. Grabbing

at his chest, the man sagged to his knees, blood coating his fingers and staining the pale blue of his shirt. In a minute, he would be dead. No one survived a gunshot wound to the heart. Not like this.

Walter spun, searching for the next threat. It came so fast. Screaming, running, a flash of a knife blade.

Screw turning the flashlight off, Walter needed to see what was coming. Once again he crossed his arms, gun in his right hand, wrist braced on top of his left arm holding the light.

No waiting. No hesitation. The second shot hit its target as well as the first. Walter couldn't say whether the assailant had been black or white or tall or short. Fat or scrawny. All he saw was the knife and visions of his daughter.

His wife and Drew waited for medicine, counting on him to deliver. He couldn't let them down. Couldn't expose his family to this new life alone. The threats lurking inside that health center wouldn't be making it out alive.

No one was getting to Madison. No one would hurt his family.

He backed into the room, sweeping it with his flashlight. A conference table sat in the middle, eight or ten chairs grouped around. No one was inside. He clicked the flashlight off and reached for Peyton, dragging his limp body into the room and clear of the door.

Walter didn't breathe until the door was shut and locked and they were secure. Only then did he suck in a lungful of air and drop to check Peyton's vitals.

Still alive.

He gave the kid's face a quick smack. No response.

Blood matted around Peyton's ear, sticky and thick as it globbed in his hair. Walter pushed Peyton's hair aside, searching for the wound. When he found it, he exhaled in relief.

Although at least two inches long and still open, it was superficial at best. Peyton wouldn't bleed to death. Worse case, he had brain damage and internal hemorrhaging. Best case, a minor concussion and hope for a full recovery.

Either way, he wasn't any good to Walter for the rest of the mission. After tucking his arms under Peyton's armpits, Walter dragged him over to the door-side wall. If anyone managed to get inside the room, Peyton would be shielded behind the door when it opened.

It wasn't the best hiding place, but it was better than nothing. Walter stood and made his way back to the door. As he opened it, the stench of fresh blood crinkled his nose. Peyton's assailant sprawled across the hall, face mashed into the linoleum, blood seeping around his T-shirt.

Walter toed the man's head, lifting the dead weight up with his shoe before turning it over to get a look at his face. His flashlight beam lingered on smooth skin pocked by acne.

In death, the kid's youth eclipsed all else. Without the heft of a weapon straining his muscles and adrenaline contorting his features, he was no older than Madison. Practically a child.

A pang of regret shot through Walter, but he forced

it down. Plenty of nineteen-year-olds were deadly. He knew that firsthand. The kid might have been a college student, but that didn't mean he deserved to keep breathing. Not after almost cracking Peyton's skull without warning.

Walter stepped over the body and flashed the light down both sides of the hall. No sign of the other assailant. Walter frowned. His shot hit the target, so where was the guy? Even in the chaos of the moment, Walter, didn't miss.

There should be a trail of blood or a body or something. Some evidence of the second attacker. *Damn it.* While he'd been tending to Peyton and letting curiosity get the best of him, a knife-wielding threat disappeared. Walter ground his teeth together. He would find him. And this time, he wouldn't let him get away.

Five feet down the hall, the next door stood partially ajar. Walter kicked it open. Screw flicking the flashlight on and off or not broadcasting his position. He was done hiding. He shone the beam in every corner and crevice of what appeared to be a waiting room. Nothing.

Turning back around, he hurried to the dead man in the hall and grabbed him by the ankle. He hauled him into the room, leaving a smear of tacky blood in his wake. As soon as the guy's head cleared the door, Walter dropped his legs and stepped over the body and back out into the hall.

He shut the door and exhaled. Hiding all the blood wasn't possible, but at least he could keep the sight of a dead man from his daughter. She didn't need to see what he had done. She didn't need to know how far he would go to protect her. Not yet.

With the gun and flashlight back in position, Walter made his way down the hall, clearing every room Madison and Brianna should have been inside by now. If they had been captured or taken hostage…

Walter's grip on the gun tightened, the checkering digging into the skin of his palm. Inhaling, he forced his body to relax. Getting choked up now wouldn't do any good. At the next door, he read the sign. Suite 107. The pharmacy had to be close.

He tried the handle. Locked. The first locked door on the inside of the building. Walter bounced the beam of light up and down the hall before flicking it off. It could be a supply closet or doctor's office or any number of things. Or it could be where the wounded knife-man was hiding.

If he ignored it and went on, he'd be leaving a potential threat behind. If he took the time to pick the lock, he'd be risking Madison and Brianna's life. They could be in the pharmacy right now or already trapped. He hated to leave the room unchecked, but he needed to clear the rest of the floor.

Against his instincts, Walter kept walking.

Suite 108. The pharmacy.

Unlike the other doors, this one had a window in the middle, although it did little good in the dark. He eased the door open, flashing the light once again like a firefly, on and off in quick, disparate bursts.

A large waiting room, a counter with three separate

areas divided by partitions to counsel customers, and rows upon rows of undisturbed medicine beyond.

Walter strode toward the counter, intermittently flashing the light held just below the gun, scouting for the man he'd shot but not killed. So far, so good. He hopped the desk and landed on the other side.

Madison was right about the difference between college hospitals and health centers. For a campus facility, the pharmacy was small. No more than fifteen rows of shelves, each about ten feet deep. Walter scanned the first aisle with his flashlight. Sudafed of every variety, epipens, a billion different boxes of birth control.

Walter shook his head. College today.

He eased into the next aisle when the sound of pill bottles clattering to the floor made him freeze. He wasn't alone.

Walter clicked off the flashlight and backed up out of the aisle until his backside brushed the cabinets on the far wall. The noise came from his left, toward the front of the pharmacy. He wished he had some night vision goggles or a red cover for the flashlight. Anything to preserve his night vision.

But he didn't. Without using the white light of the flashlight, he was blind. Walter clicked it on again, flicking it around to hopefully catch a glimpse of something. No such luck.

He'd have to ferret the person out. Rolling his feet as he walked to minimize the sound, Walter eased toward the source of the noise. His heart picked up, once again drumming in time with the adrenaline coursing through his veins.

After flicking his light on and off and glancing down a few empty aisles, Walter paused. He would never find a person this way. He sucked in a deep breath before calling out. "Is anyone here?"

No response.

"I won't shoot if you're unarmed." He walked closer to the end of the pharmacy. "Identify yourself."

At last, a labored voice called out. "I don't have a weapon. Please don't shoot."

Walter turned the flashlight back on, clearing every aisle until he reached the last one. A college kid sat on the floor, one hand pressing a wadded up fistful of gauze into his bicep.

Guess my aim wasn't perfect that time.

Walter looked him over. "Where's your knife?"

The kid couldn't have been older than twenty, the gunshot screwing up his boyish looks into a mask of pain. "I-I don't know. I must have dropped it."

"Is there anyone else in the building?"

"Just Trip, and you shot him already!"

Walter had the feeling the kid was telling the truth, but he couldn't be sure. Now, he could never be sure about anything. Another ten guys could be hiding around the corner. They could have his daughter already. They could be…

He shook off the spiraling fears and stepped closer. "Are you sure there's no one else here?"

"I'm not lying."

"How do I know that? You attacked us for no reason."

The kid's mouth screwed up into a tight, little pucker. "This is our place. We were here first."

Walter lifted his gun and the light, blinding the kid with the beam as he stepped closer.

With the toe of his shoe, Walter kicked the kid's hand out of the way before finding the entry point of the bullet. A through-and-through. He'd live. Even after a little coercion.

Walter shoved the toe of his shoe into the wound and the kid screamed. "Tell me the truth. Is there anyone else in here?"

"No!"

Walter pressed harder. Tears leaked out of the corners of the kid's eyes and he shook his head back and forth.

"Are you sure?"

"Yes! I'm sure! It's just us! Ahhh, that hurts!"

"What's you're name?"

"R-Robert."

"Your full name."

"Robert… ungh… Robert Duncan Jackson."

"Where do your parents live, Robert?"

The kid hesitated and Walter dug his toe in a bit deeper.

"At 837 Linecaster Road. Modesto."

As Walter kept the pressure on, the kid devolved into whimpering and sobbing. If he'd been lying, he would have owned up to it by now. At last, he eased back and the kid rolled onto his side, clutching his wounded arm and groaning.

"If you ever attempt to come after me or my family, I'll hunt down your parents and kill them. Slowly. Do you understand?"

Robert nodded. "Y-Yes, sir."

"Good." Walter shifted the grip on the handgun and leaned over the kid. "Now go to sleep."

As the butt of the gun made contact with Robert's head, a voice he recognized called out.

"Dad? Dad are you in here?"

DAY NINE

CHAPTER EIGHT

MADISON

863 Dewberry Lane, Chico, CA
8:00 a.m.

The flashlight beam bounced across the rear wall and Madison froze. Her father leaned over a heap of a person on the floor, hand pulled back, gun drawn. His jaw ticked and Madison let out a shout. "Dad, no!"

Madison landed hard on the wood floor, sliding right off the dining room chair as she jolted herself awake. Every time she fell asleep, the same dream replayed in her head: her father taking the student health center by storm.

As soon as they heard the first gunshot, Brianna jumped over the railing, grabbed a rock, and smashed the side window. But even then, they had taken too long.

Madison glanced over the back of the couch at

Peyton, still groggy and discombobulated in a living room chair. The side of his head swelled like a lumpy pumpkin left too long on one side. But despite the nasty bruise and clotting wound, he was lucky. Had the impact been to his temple and not a few inches higher, he would be lying on the floor of the student health center, cold and dead.

Somewhere inside, she knew her father did what he thought was necessary, but she still wondered. If they hadn't walked into the pharmacy right then, would he have killed that kid?

The sound of stairs creaking caught her ear and Madison turned to see her mom round the corner with a tired smile. "Good morning, honey. Did you sleep all right?"

Madison nodded and tried to shake off her concerns. "I took the early morning shift so Brianna could sleep. She's in the back bedroom."

Much larger than her parents' bungalow, the house they temporarily called camp held a living room and dining room open to the kitchen, and a study, bedroom, and bathroom on the first floor. With four more bedrooms upstairs it was a veritable mansion.

Her mom pulled out a dining room chair and sat down across from Madison. She motioned to Drew and Peyton. "How did they do in the night?"

"Fine. Drew seems a bit better. That IV is working."

Her mom leaned over to catch a glance. "Still not empty?"

"This one is just fluid. He took the antibiotic hours ago."

"What about Peyton?"

"His wound looks good. I don't think he needs stitches." Madison pulled a leg up and tucked it underneath her as she thought about the night before. "How's your hand?"

"Better. The burn ointment you found is helping and the antibiotics already seem to be working. The worst area is oozing less this morning."

Madison glanced at the stacks of medicine lined up on the counter. "How did Dad know what types of medicine to grab?"

Her mom shrugged. "We've both taken some advanced CPR and first aid classes over the years. When we were backpacking a lot, he even took some wilderness EMT courses." She moved to the end of the table and picked up the first box. "This is Moxifloxacin, it's a good all-around antibacterial agent. It's effective against everything from Staph to pneumonia to tuberculosis. It might even work against MRSA."

Madison shook her head. "I've never even heard of it. How do you know so much about it?"

Her mom smiled. "I have a lot of free time at the library."

"So you read medical guides?"

"Sort of. When we took that week-long trip to Alaska, I read up on everything from bear safety to emergency medicine. I wanted to take a solid emergency medical kit with us, since we were airlifted in all by ourselves. A lot can happen in the two days it could have taken a ranger to find us."

Madison exhaled. She felt like such a novice

compared to everyone around her. Brianna knew her way around weapons like they were place settings, and Tucker could explain everything from solar weather to how the internet might come back soon. Her dad could fly and shoot anything. And her mom was a walking repository of key information.

What could she possibly hope to contribute to their new way of life? When it came down to it, she couldn't even make the hard choices.

"What is it, honey?"

She glanced up at her mom. Even with greasy hair and no makeup, her mom was so beautiful. Pale skin, blue eyes, hair only a little bit gray. Every wrinkle was a reminder of all her mom's life experience. All of her skills and knowledge.

Madison glanced down at the table and ran her fingers over the grain in the wood. "I feel so unprepared for all of this. Like I've been living in some fantasy land my whole life and I've just woken up."

A knot in the table top caught her fingernail and Madison traced its warbled circle around and around until she hit the center. "I should have done more. Learned more. Instead I goofed off and had fun." Her eyebrows tucked in as she shoved her nail into the wood. "I'm weak."

Her mom's good hand landed on top of her own, the hardened bumps of new calluses pressing into her skin. "You are no such thing. Look at all that you've accomplished in such a short time. You made it all the way from school to home. You helped us save as much as we could from the house."

With a squeeze of her hand, her mom paused. "Most importantly, you're alive. That's what matters the most. We've all come from different places and seen and experienced different things."

Madison sniffed. "I could have tried harder."

"Think about all the things you do know. Eventually all the running will stop. We'll find a place to settle down and thanks to you and Peyton, we'll be able to grow vegetables and fruit, and maybe even raise some animals."

"You really think so?"

"Right now is just a time of transition. At some point, everything will stabilize. It has to."

Madison swallowed. "What if it doesn't? What if this right here is as good as it gets?"

Her mom pulled back, her fingers trailing across the wood like a receding tide of warmth and hope. "Then we fight. We're not giving up, Madison. No matter how hard it gets, we're going to make it."

Madison leaned back and pulled her limp, grimy hair off her face. It had been so long since she'd washed it; she'd become accustomed to the thick texture of dirt and oil all mixed together.

She thought about all the things she took for granted before and now lived without: showers, hot food, a bed, a home. Stability and safety. The genuine goodness of her fellow man.

"Do you think there are other people like us out there?"

"What do you mean?"

Madison tried to put her swirling thoughts into

words. "Normal people. Not the ones who instantly think about robbing and stealing or the ones sitting on their hands waiting for someone else to help them. But people like us, trying to survive the best way we can."

"Yes." Her mom's eyes lit with an intensity when she spoke that Madison couldn't help but believe her. "I do. Of course when times get tough, some people revert to their baser instincts and some just give up. But there are plenty of good people out there in this country who see the loss of power as a temporary hardship. People who will survive without losing sight of what makes us human."

Her mom reached back out and patted Madison's hand. "People just like us."

Madison stared at their hands, one wrinkled but strong, the other smooth and unsure. "What if people like us don't make it? What do we do then?"

"We make the best of it." Her mom pushed back her chair and motioned toward the kitchen. "I checked last night and the gas is still running for the stove. How about we find the pantry and see if we can't make some drop biscuits? I could go for some fresh-cooked food."

Madison glanced around her. "We're already using the house. You don't feel bad about eating the food?"

"The couple who lives here is in New York. I found their itinerary in the study. I don't think they'll be making it back here, honey."

Madison thought about all of her friends who were trapped in the same situation. How many were in Mexico right now on a beach with no means to connect to back home? Did they even know about the blackout?

Had the EMP hit Cancun as hard as it hit the United States?

She shook her head to clear it. Wondering about the what-ifs would get her nowhere. They detoured to Chico for a reason. She glanced up at her mom. "What about the girl at the radio station?"

"If she's stuck inside that building, she'll still be there in a few hours. But we need to eat, rest, and come up with a plan of attack. We need to do this smart, not fast."

Madison pressed her lips together to keep from frowning. Part of her wanted to rush over there and break the doors down without wasting another minute, but one glance at Peyton and Drew and she knew her mother was right. They needed to be strong. Ready.

She stood up and followed her mother into the kitchen. If they could feed everyone and come up with a better plan than the one from the night before, maybe her father wouldn't have to shoulder the heaviest load.

Her mom opened the cabinet doors and let out a little yelp of satisfaction. An unopened jug of Shake 'n Pour Bisquick sat on the shelf next to the salt and baking soda. She held it up with a triumphant smile. "Forget biscuits. We're having pancakes."

"Do you think we can spare the water?"

Her mother nodded. "There's a fifty-gallon water heater in the utility closet. I'm pretty sure the people who live here left for spring break before the grid failed. If so, that means it's probably full."

Her mom's blue eyes sparkled in the morning light.

"We have enough water for pancakes, coffee, and if we can fill the bathtub—"

Madison's heart almost skipped a beat. "We can get clean?"

"And if we're lucky, use the gray water to wash some clothes."

Madison opened up the next cabinet and pulled down a glass bowl. Her mother was right. Pancakes, a bath, and clean clothes would do more to improve their moods than any rushed plan of attack. They could take a few hours to rest and recover and monitor Drew and Peyton. The radio station wasn't going anywhere.

She set the bowl on the counter with a smile. "What are we waiting for? Let's get cooking."

CHAPTER NINE

TRACY

863 Dewberry Lane, Chico, CA
12:00 p.m.

The sound of laughter brought a stillness to Tracy's insides. A certain calm came from a morning spent in normalcy—washing clothes, cooking breakfast, enjoying good company. It was fleeting. The sun would advance across the sky, the evening would come on, and darkness would descend like a thick wool blanket.

Gone were the streaks of green and blue that lit up the night for the first few days after the solar storm. In their place, darkness reigned.

In the abstract, she could handle the lack of power. They had camped in remote enough places that the absence of artificial light didn't bother her. But nothing could prepare them for the threat the darkness brought.

Fear. Dread. A sweat-slicked anticipation that

someone out there in the night wanted to do them harm. After the fire, Tracy wasn't sure she would ever sleep soundly again.

"Had I known how many beans we'd eat after the apocalypse, I would have spent some more time learning how to cook them." Madison sighed as she held up two cans. "Green beans or peas?"

Brianna groaned. "Have you ever smelled a canned pea? It's like a combination of vomit and rotting garden."

"Well now that you've won me over, peas it is!" Tucker snatched the can of peas from Madison's hand and tossed it back and forth as he walked over to the kitchen counter.

"I'm warning you Tucker, your breakfast will come right back up if you open that." Brianna stood in the door of the pantry, hands on her hips as she stared at her boyfriend.

Tracy held in her laugh. Watching Tucker and Brianna give each other grief reminded her of the past, when Walter was a young college student out to win her over, and she was too focused on learning to give him the time of day.

She smiled and caught her husband's eye. "Do you remember that time you tried to cook me dinner?"

His eyes lit up. "Which one?"

"You know. In Albuquerque."

Walter held up his hands. "In my defense, I had no idea bell peppers were hollow."

"You're joking." Madison turned to her parents and looked first at her dad and then Tracy. "Right, Mom?"

Tracy let a small laugh escape. "Not a chance. Before he met me, your father wasn't much for cooking." She walked over and slipped an arm around his middle. "But he still makes a mean PB&J, all these years later."

He leaned in and kissed Tracy's temple. "It's the cinnamon raisin bread. That's the secret."

"Aww, man. People really eat these?" A can clattered onto the counter and Tucker staggered back, clutching his midsection and his nose at the same time.

Brianna smiled in triumph. "Told you so."

"Hey, don't knock the canned peas. If we don't find a place to settle down and start a homestead, that might be the closest thing to a vegetable we're going to get." Walter stepped forward and grabbed the can, inhaling deep as he stuck his nose into the open top. "Not as bad as tray-rat sausage. You want to smell foul? That would be it."

"The more you talk about the Marine Corps, Mr. Sloane, the happier I am I never enlisted."

Walter shrugged. "It wasn't all bad. I can fly a Hornet at Mach 1.8." His smile fell and he sagged a bit against the counter. "At least I could before."

A hush fell over everyone as the reminder of their future killed the good mood. Tracy held her hand out for the can. "There's a couple cans of tuna and some mayo in the pantry. You'll never taste the peas when I mix it all up."

Her husband nodded. "Madison, can you check the garage for any more supplies? Sometimes people store their extra shelf-stable stuff out there. Brianna, there's a half a case of bottled water in the pantry. We can drink it. Tucker, can you search for a portable radio? If there's one around here somewhere, we can check on the girl broadcasting and see if she's still there."

Everyone dispersed and Walter smiled at his wife. "How are you?"

"Better. The medicine you found is working. My hand only hurts once in a while now."

"Good." He stepped closer and dropped his voice. "If we go after that girl, you'll have to stay here, you know that, right?"

Tracy hesitated. Deep down, she did, but it still stung. "Someone has to watch Peyton and Drew, and I suppose it should be me."

"You're the only one who can't use both her hands." Walter took her injured hand in his and turned it palm up. The worst of the wounds stopped weeping that morning, but the skin still refused to scab. "It will be dangerous. Worse than the student health center."

"About that—" Tracy still hadn't convinced Walter to open up about what happened there. From the blood on his clothes and the haunted look in his eye, she guessed he'd made some tough choices.

"We can talk about it later. Suffice it to say, we're lucky no one died."

"You mean not one of us." Brianna strode back into the room, an open case of water in her hands.

Her husband didn't answer and Tracy's eyes went wide. "Is she right, Walt? Did you have to kill someone?"

He glanced at Brianna. "How did you know?"

She exhaled, her shoulders lowering as she thought over how to answer. "You don't strike me as the bygones type. After what happened to Peyton, I figured you took care of whatever threat presented itself." Brianna turned and set the water on the counter. "Am I wrong?"

Walter shook his head. "No. You're not."

"Good. Because whoever tried to kill Peyton deserved whatever they got."

Tracy knew Brianna shared the same type of ethos as her husband, a sort of warped golden rule where another's actions determined their fate. "Have you changed your mind about this rescue attempt?"

Brianna scoffed. "No. It's a terrible idea."

"But you'll do it?"

She glanced at Tracy before answering Walter. "Yes. But only because it matters to Madison. If she changes her mind, I'm fine with it. We have the medicine, we've had a chance to stop moving and clean up and eat. So far, the benefits have outweighed the costs."

"But?"

"At some point, those scales will tilt the other way and I'll regret ever stepping foot on Chico State's campus."

Tucker spoke up from the entry to the hall. "Found a radio. If we're going in, we should do it soon. She's sounding pretty desperate."

Tracy steeled herself. All too soon, her husband and daughter would be leaving her again. She just hoped they would once again make it back.

CHAPTER TEN

MADISON

Parking lot, CSU Chico
4:00 p.m.

Madison replayed Mandy Patterson's last broadcast over and over in her head as they staked out the communications building. She'd claimed their water and food had run out and that one of her friends wouldn't wake up.

If there was even a chance she told the truth, then Madison couldn't turn her back. They might not be able to take Mandy and her friends with them to Brianna's cabin, but they could at least save them from certain death locked in a building.

She crouched down next to her father as he used the binoculars she had purchased at the sporting goods store in Davis before the CME hit. "I see no activity from the outside. It's a black box as far as we know. There are five entry and exit points, one of which is on the roof."

"Where do you think she's broadcasting from?"

Tucker pointed at the radio tower. "The booth she's using is probably in a direct line from the tower, just to save on component and cabling costs."

"It's a one-story building, so we're looking at somewhere in the middle of it. If it's anything like the radio stations I've seen on TV, it'll have glass walls and plenty of equipment inside."

Tucker nodded. "That's right. Even college campus radio stations are built like the real thing. Their broadcast reach isn't as far, but they have all the capabilities of a full-scale commercial station."

"How do you know so much about radio stations?"

"I had a vintage transistor radio as a kid and played with it all the time. You can pick up AM stations from hundreds of miles away."

Madison nodded. She did the same thing. "All right. So we all go in together. Which entrance?"

Her father lowered the binoculars and pointed. "The west side. It's only one door, and appears to enter into a hall or vestibule. That'll be our best bet. It's far enough away from the broadcasting booth that we can get inside without being right on top of them. And with only one door, there's not as much to defend if we have to retreat."

Madison exhaled, her breath shaky as adrenaline kicked in. She knew this was risky. She knew she was asking her dad and her friends to put their lives on the line for a stranger. "Thank you all for coming with me. I know it's dangerous. But I can't leave her here."

Brianna shifted beside her and checked to ensure her shotgun was loaded and ready. "We'll always have your back, Madison. Even when you're being an idiot."

Madison managed a small smile. "Thanks."

"Let's do this before it gets any later. I want to use the daylight to our advantage. No more breaking into unknown buildings in the dark." Her father pointed at the tree line. "If we keep to the trees until we're past the door and circle back, they won't see us coming. There's no windows over there."

He shoved the binoculars into a pocket of his pants. "Let's do this. First sign of trouble, we retreat, understood?"

Everyone agreed.

Ten minutes later, Madison stood behind her father, scoping out the parking lot as he tried the door handle. Locked. At least that part of her story was panning out.

"You think it's locked from the inside?"

"Only way to find out is to break in. Give me five minutes; it looks easy."

True to his word, her father unlocked the door in a handful of minutes with nothing more than a pair of paper clips. Yet another example of a skill Madison wished she'd learned.

He turned the handle, but Madison reached out to stop him. "I love you, Dad."

"I love you, too. Now get ready. We're going to get this girl and get the hell out."

Madison's father eased the door open and the

sunlight from outside cast a ray of light down an empty hall. "Prop the door open. At least that way we'll have a rendezvous point."

Brianna shoved a rock underneath the bottom of the door and wedged it open. "Done."

"Then let's go. Single file, everyone behind me."

Madison's hands shook as she held a shotgun in her hands. The butt of the gun dug into her shoulder as she pressed it tight, trying in vain to quell her nerves.

All she could see inside was the shaft of light. The hall seemed to stretch on forever, leading into a cavern of dim open space and what could have been a wall of windows beyond. How would they ever find the broadcast booth?

The hair on her neck rose as her father stepped into the communications building and momentarily disappeared. Madison rushed to keep up with him, gun raised and ready. Maybe it would all work out. Maybe they wouldn't be walking into a trap.

Every step they took deeper into the building, her fear and regret rose, threatening to close her throat in panic. *Why did I insist on coming here? Why are we doing this?* Her breath came in shallow bursts, in, in, out, out. Her cheeks flushed hot, fingers trembling as the grip of the shotgun slipped against her palm.

Brianna eased up beside her. "Just keep walking. It'll be okay."

Madison nodded and took another step. Her father had cleared the first portion of the hall, trying door handles and opening the rooms that gave, ignoring the ones that were locked.

"Do you want me to go ahead?"

Madison nodded again. "Yes. I'll be right behind you."

"Okay."

She watched as Brianna eased past her and hurried to catch up to her father. Together the two of them worked as a team, one opening a door while the other swept a gun and flashlight over the room.

Watching the pair of them work so efficiently brought a modicum of calm to Madison's mind. Maybe they could do this. Maybe it would all work out.

Madison followed her father and roommate to the end of the hall with Tucker on her heels. The building opened up before them in a large waiting area. The windows Madison spotted when they first opened the building door sat straight ahead. She squinted, unable to make out the interior without light.

Tucker pulled out his flashlight and walked past her. Easing up to the dark windows, he made eye contact with Madison's father. As soon as her father nodded, Tucker turned on the light and lit up the broadcast booth.

Empty.

A lump crashed into Madison's stomach, churning in a sea of acid as she stared at the empty space. Was Mandy somewhere else inside the building or was the whole thing a trap?

She backed up, retracing her steps to the directory she passed ten feet back. If she read the map, maybe they could figure out where else she could be. A cafeteria or break room. Maybe a green room for guests.

Madison never saw the shadows shift behind her or the looming shape materialize out of the dark. By the time the hand wrapped around her mouth, a knife point lodged into the soft space beneath her chin. The blade dug into the unprotected flesh, deep enough to draw blood, but not slice an artery.

Lips landed hot on her ear, stubble scratching against her naked lobe. "If you scream, I kill you. If you try to hurt me, I kill you. If you try to escape, I kill you. Understand?"

She nodded into the blade, wincing as it cut a bit deeper.

"Good. Now back up." The man who held her pulled with the hand around her mouth, half-dragging Madison further into the dark. Panic threatened to overwhelm her. Hot, burning tears filled her eyes and clouded her vision. *This is all my fault.*

She blinked against the temporary blindness, willing Tucker or her father or Brianna to see her. They were all busy with the broadcast booth, scoping it out while she was meant to keep the rear secure.

In seconds, she would be too far away to see, too far gone to do any good. The last week replayed in her head. All the times she doubted herself and gave other people too much credit. When things had gone right, she had stepped up and taken charge. *Done something.*

When she stood by and let the world lead, only pain and regret followed. Where would they be if Brianna had listened to her and not followed the semi-truck off the causeway? Where would they be if they had killed the man who broke into their house instead of tying him up and talking it out?

Before the power grid failed, structure and rules and propriety held people together. Madison could take her time and be content to watch from the sidelines. She could be weak.

But now?

The man dragged her toward an open doorway, twisting her around as he angled into the space. His belly pressed into her back, pudgy and thick, and the scent of stale beer hit her nose as they neared the door.

She couldn't let him take her. She couldn't let him get inside or she may never make it out.

Madison shifted her grip on the shotgun. Why he hadn't taken it, she had no idea. Maybe he couldn't figure out how without removing the knife, or maybe he thought she would scream without a hand on her mouth. Either way, it gave her an opportunity.

She couldn't waste it. Not this time.

With her teeth clenched tight, Madison braced for the knife's blade as she twisted in the man's grasp. She jabbed the butt of the shotgun back past her side and directly into his soft middle.

The man grunted from the impact, the hand around her mouth shifted, and the knife dug deeper into her neck. Madison opened her mouth and bit down, digging her teeth into the knuckles of two fingers.

Blood welled across her tongue, bright and tangy and she bit harder as she twisted, the knife cutting across her throat like an arc of lightning searing her skin.

The pain gave her focus and courage and Madison

broke free, stumbling back as she brought the shotgun back up. It was cocked and loaded. No more hesitation. No more doubt. This man she could barely see in the dark had tried to take her away from her family He'd used her sympathy to lure them here.

She wasn't going to be a fish on a hook. She wouldn't take the bait.

The shotgun blast boomed through the hall, sending a giant, reverberating echo through the building. Madison's attacker groaned and fell to his knees. Madison fired again. In the flare of the shot, she watched the man's face explode.

Muffled shouts sounded from down the hall followed by the vibrations of footsteps on the hard floor. A flashlight beam bounced and wobbled closer and closer until her father stuttered to a stop a few feet away.

The light landed on the dead man five feet in front of Madison and then flicked up to her face. She couldn't see anything but the light.

CHAPTER ELEVEN

WALTER

COMMUNICATIONS BUILDING, CSU CHICO
6:00 p.m.

MADISON. WALTER MOVED THE FLASHLIGHT AWAY FROM her face. Blood spatter pocked her hands and stained her clothes, but it wasn't the carnage that twisted Walter's insides.

It was the look in his daughter's eyes. The cold detachment, a body removed from the mind, stuck in a never-ending loop of horror and static.

She wasn't supposed to be here in this moment, experiencing this fresh evil. The world should be keeping her safe. *I should be keeping her safe.*

If anyone should be killing people, it should have been Walter. The man trained to fight and defend and keep his country safe. The man who took an oath to protect and swore to defend. Not a nineteen-year-old girl who a week ago bent over tomato plants in a greenhouse without a care in the world.

Madison should be making friends and falling in love and learning all about the joy and wonder of life. Not standing in a dark hallway staring down at a man she killed.

I failed her.

Walter reached for the gun and pried it out of his daughter's hands. He remembered her first wobbly steps across the living room in their old house and the first time she said Daddy. The first day of school and first bike ride. First school dance and first date.

Now he could add first kill.

Brianna rushed up to his side, gun tracking the empty hall. "We need to clear the room. If he intended to drag Madison inside, there's probably more of them." Her nose wrinkled as the copper tang of death hit her nose. "I knew it was a trap."

Walter handed Madison's shotgun to Brianna. "Take this. I'll clear the room."

"Do you need—"

He didn't give the teenager time to finish. No, he didn't need any help. Not now. Screw holding back. Screw trying to do the right thing. The new world didn't give a damn whether the innocent lived or died or had to do the unthinkable.

After checking the handgun he carried still held a full magazine, Walter reached for the rifle slung across his back. In tight quarters he preferred the ease of the handgun. Concealment, weapon retention, and lethality with lower risk of penetrating a wall or shooting an innocent bystander.

But now none of that mattered. He would clear this building and kill everything that breathed. The handgun fit snugly inside his waistband and the rifle was wedged securely against his shoulder. One deep breath and he was as ready as he would ever get.

Walter leaned close to his daughter and planted a kiss on her temple. "Don't worry, honey. Everything is going to be all right."

He turned to Brianna who waited across the hall in the pale shaft of light from the still-open door. "Stay here until I clear a room, then barricade yourselves in. Don't come out until you hear my call."

"A cardinal?"

"That's the one."

Brianna closed the distance between herself and Madison, gun ready, eyes alert.

Walter gave her a nod and clicked on the small flashlight he'd taped to the barrel of the rifle.

Three, two, one.

He stepped over the dead body clogging up the entrance to the room and pushed the door wide as he scanned the room. A flutter of movement caught his eye behind an overturned table. Was that a scrap of fabric? The edge of a hat brim?

Didn't matter.

Pull. Pull. Pull.

Walter fired three rounds into the table. From fifteen feet away, the high-velocity round dug through the wood and spit out the other side like a kid landing a cannonball in the deep end of a pool.

A grunt and a slump and a muffled scream. A hand flopped onto the floor, dangling and dead.

One down.

He tracked the scuffling of another body behind the table. Another casualty whose heart hadn't stopped yet.

Walter pulled the trigger another three times.

A second one bit the dust. Or, more accurately, the grimy linoleum of a student-run communications building. Give it a few years and the dust would settle, but for now there was more blood and misery than dust.

Blinking to wet his eyes, Walter stepped further into the room. No more movement. Were there only three of them? Why would they broadcast if their ranks were so thin? What did they hope to accomplish?

No. There had to be more somewhere else. That meant Madison and her friends were still in danger. He needed to speed up and eliminate the threat for good.

Walter cleared the room in efficient grace, sweeping every nook and cranny almost like a MARSOC operator on patrol. It wasn't an air strike with designated targets and bomb drops, but taking out the enemy up close and personal engendered a similar rush.

Adrenaline and fear and pride. War was a perverse enterprise.

He paused to assess the dead. One woman, two men, if he included the one in the entryway. Too old to be college kids. If the brunette with a tattoo snaking over her shoulder and track marks up her arm was the radio star, Mandy Patterson hadn't seen a college class in years.

Meth or heroin were her star subjects. Not communications, nor broadcasting, nor agriculture.

On some level, Walter had always known the end of the world would give strength to the fringe of society. An addict stood a better chance of surviving and adapting than a normal person.

They were used to hunger and base need. Hustle and manipulation. Doing the hard thing if it got them what they needed.

Had this group already tried to break in to the pharmacy? Were they kept out by the very people Walter took out at the health center?

Walter kicked at the torso of the woman. Her mouth fell open to reveal rotting teeth, half gray and black and reeking of decay. A drug addict's downfall would be the very thing that kept them alive. Without ready access to dealers and drugs, how long could they last?

The enterprising could learn to make their own. With enough pharmacies and chemicals around, meth could still be produced for a while. When it ran out…

They would perish, but only after wreaking as much havoc as they could. Walter crouched beside the woman and bit back his disgust. At least he would end this.

After searching her for weapons and anything useful, he moved on to the man beside her. Same sullen skin and sunken eye sockets. Same bad teeth and scars from prolonged drug use. Such a waste.

Walter searched him as well, pocketing a lighter but finding nothing else of value. He stood and made his way to the man his daughter killed. The one who almost took his baby away from him.

The one thing he lived for more than anything in this world. He would go to the ends of the earth to protect Madison. He bent beside the body, avoiding the now-congealing pool of blood. Fishing in the man's pockets, Walter struck gold.

A ring of keys. He held them up, using the flashlight to read the label. *Communications Building.*

Bingo. With the keys on his belt and his rifle at the ready, Walter walked back out of the room. After checking to make sure Brianna still stood guard over Madison and Tucker, he cleared the next room.

"This room is clear." He motioned for the kids to follow him. "Stay here. I'll be back when I know the building is secure."

Brianna ushered Tucker and Madison inside before turning around. "Do you need any help?"

"No. I need you to stay here."

Brianna nodded.

Madison frowned as she sat down in an empty conference chair, her eyes still cloudy and troubled. In the dim light, the blood blended into her face and she looked almost clean. "Be careful, Dad."

"I will."

Walter exited the room and waited until he heard the click of the door lock before exhaling. The kids were safe. He could clear the rest of the building without worrying about them.

The rest of the hall went by in a blur with keys and empty rooms and quiet. He shut the door to the outside and turned to face the interior once more. Based on the map he'd passed, there were only a handful of rooms left.

Walter worked in calm precision, his heart slowing to normal levels as it became evident they were alone. At last, he unlocked the broadcast booth and stepped inside.

The stench of death hit him hard and fast and Walter brought his arm up to his face to shield his nose from the smell. Scanning the room with his flashlight, his heart sank as he landed on the source.

A young woman lay in a heap on the floor, half of her head bashed in, dried blood crusting and flaking from her ashen face. Walter stepped forward and bent to read the ID card hanging from a lanyard around her neck.

Mandy Patterson
Junior, CSU, Chico

He swallowed. Madison was right. Mandy was real and they were too late. His daughter wasn't the only one who took the chance on finding Mandy and her friends alive. Only the people who came to rescue them weren't their saviors, but their destruction.

Walter stood up and searched the rest of the room, coming up empty. He didn't know whether the others had escaped or were killed and dumped somewhere else. It didn't matter now. Whatever chance Mandy had was gone.

At least he'd killed the people who must have been responsible. Walter said a brief prayer and slung his rifle back over his shoulder before bending to pick her up. He would take her somewhere, lay her to rest as best he could, and go back for Madison and her friends.

They couldn't save Mandy, but maybe, with Tucker's help, they could find out what the hell was going on in the rest of the world. A single green light glowed on the panel of controls and knobs in the booth.

The label read, *Solar Ready*.

After all that had happened that day, that one little blip of light gave Walter hope.

CHAPTER TWELVE

MADISON

Communications Building, CSU Chico
7:00 p.m.

Madison wiped her neck, her own blood tightening as it dried on her skin. If they made it out of the communications building alive, she would find a way to take a shower. This blood would come off. It wouldn't define her.

Brianna eased down into the chair next to her. "Are you all right?"

Madison glanced over at the roommate to whom she'd never given enough credit. "Yeah. How about you?"

"All things considered, I'm all right."

"But?"

Brianna kicked at a scuff on the floor. "I should be

out there helping your dad. He shouldn't be clearing a building this large on his own."

"He's trying to protect you."

"He should know by now that I'm capable of protecting myself."

Madison frowned. "Aren't you scared? Don't you question what we're doing and what's going on out there that we don't know about?"

Brianna sat the shotgun on the table behind her and turned back around. She smiled at her boyfriend who sat at the other end of the conference table, fiddling with audio equipment he found in the cabinet on the far wall.

At last, she answered. "I haven't stopped to think about it. I can't until we make it to the cabin and I talk to my mom and dad."

Madison remembered the fear and worry that dominated her thoughts before she reunited with her family. To have that linger and stretch on for weeks… It would have driven her mad. That Brianna channeled it all into this commando girl, able to fight and kill and do anything to survive, made sense in a way.

But it still didn't quell the rising tide within Madison. She reached behind her and picked up the shotgun Brianna discarded on the table. If she looked carefully enough, she could make out the spatter of blood from her first kill.

"Do you regret it?"

Brianna's question caught her off-guard and she glanced up. "Killing someone? No."

She turned the gun over in her hands as she tried to

put the teeming ocean of her thoughts into words. "My dad thinks I'm an innocent kid, someone who needs protecting. And in a way, I've acted like that. Unsure what to do, brave one minute and terrified the next."

"That's to be expected. We're not soldiers, Madison."

"I know. But that's not why I froze back there. I shot that man because I had to. If I didn't he'd have cut my throat." She reached up to run her fingers once more along the wound at her neck. The bleeding had stopped quickly, but the gash still hurt.

"I froze because in that moment it hit me: this is the best it's ever going to get. This right here."

A clang made Madison jump. Tucker eased out of the chair at the end of the table and reached for a metal spring that rolled across the floor. "You can't think that. This isn't forever. Humans are resilient. The power loss is only a temporary setback."

Madison smiled at Tucker's optimism, but she no longer shared it. "I wish I could believe you. But I can't. Not anymore. Look at everything that's happened to us. Wanda is dead. Drew lost his fiancée and is seriously injured. Peyton is still recovering. And we've been lucky."

"I wouldn't call getting your house burned down lucky."

Brianna spoke up. "I agree with Tucker. Sure, we could have faced worse, but we're alive because we've been smart and vigilant, not because of luck."

"Fine. Maybe I haven't given us enough credit, but still. No one is coming to help us. No one is going to put society back together. Everything is breaking down." Madison rubbed at her bruised shoulder from the shotgun blast. "We're never going to be safe again."

Tucker leaned back in his chair, focusing on the acoustic ceiling panels as he spoke. "I'm not giving up hope. Until we hear from the government or find out what's going on in the rest of the country, I'll be optimistic. For all we know, the East Coast has power. The federal government could be mobilizing right now."

"No way." Brianna shook her head until a few stray curls sprang free. "We would have heard or seen something."

"You know how slow the government is to do anything. It could take months for aid to reach us from across the country." Tucker tucked his shaggy hair behind his ear. "I'm not giving up until we have proof."

Madison opened her mouth to respond when three short chirps interrupted. "Dad!" She jumped up and rushed to the door, unlocking it and pulling it wide as quickly as possible.

Her father stood in the doorway with an unreadable expression. "The building is clear." He glanced down at the shotgun still in her hand and frowned. "Are you okay?"

Madison nodded. "Did you find anyone else?"

He stepped into the room, shoulders drooping and aging him a decade in a single breath. "We were too late."

A block of cement wedged in Madison's throat.

"Mandy was real?" It was Tucker's turn to voice the fears they all felt inside.

Madison's father nodded. "I don't know if she was with the people who attacked us, but it doesn't seem likely. She had a CSU Chico ID. The others…" His lips quirked in disgust. "Meth heads, most likely. They won't be a problem anymore."

"What about Mandy's friends? She said on the broadcast there were five of them."

Her father rubbed his hand over his head, mussing up the strands. "No sign of them. She could have been lying in an effort to dissuade thugs from finding her. Five college kids are harder to overpower than one. Or they could have fled. I don't know."

He raised his head and met Madison's stare. "I'm sorry I doubted you, honey. We should have come sooner."

Madison shook her head. "Don't apologize. You were right. We shouldn't have come. It was a mistake."

"No, it wasn't." Her father's face brightened for the first time since stepping into the room. "Everyone grab your things. I've found something."

Thirty minutes later, Madison, her father, and Brianna all crowded around Tucker as he worked the radio controls. Madison couldn't begin to understand half of the lingo Tucker spewed out as he flipped switches and pushed buttons, but it didn't matter if he could turn the radio booth into a receiver.

"You really think this will work?"

"Yes. The antenna on the roof is massive. If I can just figure this out, we should be able to pick up anyone broadcasting on the West Coast. We might reach a whole lot farther. Hold on."

Tucker rotated a knob and flipped another switch. "I'm betting if anyone is broadcasting, it's over AM, but we'll pick up a bunch of interference since the sun has set. And if the effects of the space weather are still in the atmosphere, who knows what we'll get."

Madison rubbed a bruise forming on her shoulder. "The sun can disrupt AM radio?"

Tucker nodded without turning around. "AM radio in the United States is all short and medium wave. These types of sound waves travel in a straight line from the broadcast source until they hit the ionosphere, a layer of our atmosphere a few hundred miles above sea level."

He bent down and fiddled with a cable beneath the controls before popping back up and continuing. "During the day, the ionosphere is full of free electrons from the sun's rays, and when an AM station is broadcasting, the waves it spits out hit the lower level of the ionosphere and bounce back to the ground."

Tucker paused to flip another switch. "But at night, the sun isn't there to ionize the atmosphere, so the lower layers of the ionosphere lose enough free electrons for an AM radio wave to penetrate further. When the electrons higher up in the layer encounter an AM wave, they oscillate at the frequency of the wave."

With another push of a button, the control panel began to glow. Tucker spun around the chair with a smile on his face. "Think of it like a skywave instead of a groundwave. During the day, we're limited by the sun's effects, but at night, we can harness the atmosphere to broadcast for thousands of miles in the right conditions."

Madison shook her head. She had no idea the radio she grew up scrolling through in her parents' car and the one she listened to in the greenhouse at UC Davis was built on so much science. "Did you learn all of this in your astrophysics classes?"

Tucker shook his head. "No. My dad was a HAM radio operator. It's actually because of him that I'm into astrophysics at all." The corners of Tucker's smile slipped as he mentioned his father.

"Sorry." Madison tried not to bring up Tucker's parents. She couldn't imagine what it had been like losing the pair of them as a kid.

"It's okay." He brightened. "Let's see if this works, shall we?" Tucker turned back around and reached for a knob, turning it until a burst of static filled the station.

Madison's father patted Tucker on the back. "Good job, Tucker."

"Did you know this would work?"

Her father shrugged. "I thought it might. I'm not an expert like Tucker here, but thanks to all the international flights I've been on lately, I've learned a bit more about radio waves and how they function." He turned back to the control panel. "Now we have to hope someone is out there."

CHAPTER THIRTEEN

WALTER

COMMUNICATIONS BUILDING, CSU CHICO
9:00 p.m.

THE FIRST HINT OF STATIC TRANSFORMING INTO voices sent Walter's stomach straight into his throat.

"—inside Saddleback College. It's bad down here. Stores are all looted. Everything's either on fire or burned to the ground or smashed into bits. A bunch of military came and blocked off Los Angeles. We can't get in and they aren't letting anyone out."

Walter swallowed. He knew what those barricades were like.

"San Diego's the same way. They haven't come down as far as Mission Viejo, I guess we're not important enough." The man broadcasting let out a half-snort, half-laugh. "My friend Ricky went up to the barricades yesterday, trying to learn something about his parents inside. He got a gun pointed at him and told to back off or he'd have a bullet in his chest."

The man paused and Walter exhaled. It was the same across the entire state of California. No power. No assistance. Nothing but barricades and a bunch of national guardsmen scared shitless and without pay.

"We need help. Food and water and an explanation for what the hell happened. Where is our president? Our governor? Shouldn't they be on the radio? Shouldn't we have heard by now? We can't be the only radio station running on solar power, can we? Again, this is Jake from Saddleback College."

Tucker clicked the dial. It didn't take long to find another voice.

"—saying years. That can't be true, can it? No power for years? If it weren't for the wind turbines up here we wouldn't have anything. How will we survive without power? We're only sixty miles outside of Portland. When I stand out on my porch at night, I can still see the fires burning. Those people can't survive much longer."

The woman's voice cracked on the last word and she paused. Walter reached out and took his daughter's hand. The entire West Coast was in the dark. He'd seen it from up in the air, but he knew Madison held out hope.

"Will the government let people starve? Will they step in to help or just hide somewhere and do nothing? I can't believe this is America. We used to stand for something. Believe in something. Now…"

Tucker moved the knob and the woman's voice

faded into static. "Let's see if we can find someone farther east. I don't know how long of a charge the solar panels have. Without the sun shining, we could run out soon."

Walter nodded and waited as Tucker scrolled through more static and more voices, moving on when they determined the station was still on the West Coast.

"Wait! Go back!" Brianna spoke up for the first time in a long while. "I thought they said Chicago."

Tucker clicked back slowly until a voice filtered back through.

"The mayor declared martial law, but it's not doing any good. Every drug dealer and petty criminal in this town has a gun, but none of the good people do. We're barricaded in our homes and offices. Trapped. I heard the police are leaving. The national guard are abandoning their posts. The grocery store on the corner still has food, but the owner won't take cash. He's demanding crazy things like prescription drugs and gasoline and fuel. What twenty-something has a spare can of gasoline in his apartment?"

Walter glanced at his daughter. The muscles in her jaw twitched as she ground her teeth together. Was she angry? Sad? In shock? Walter wanted to comfort her, but he didn't know how. He squeezed her hand.

"I thought about bartering with my half bottle of Xanax, but then I wondered if maybe I shouldn't just keep it. When the food runs out, a bottle of pills and a bottle of scotch might not be a bad way to go. So much for living the good life. A job in the Loop, an apartment with a view of Lake Michigan, and I'm going to die because the power won't turn back on."

He laughed, cold and hollow. "So much for all this modern technology! My boss rigged the solar panels so that we could broadcast in the event of an emergency, but he didn't think to hook them up to anything but the damn transmitter! So here I am, a radio DJ, sitting in the dark, talking to no one until my luck runs out. This is Billy D, broadcasting from the heart of Chicago."

Tucker turned down the volume. "Now we know it's as far as Chicago."

"And it doesn't sound good." Tucker reached for Brianna's hand and held it, his eyes as full of fear and confusion as the rest of them.

Walter wished he could do something to show these kids they would make it. But he didn't know where to begin. If what all these broadcasters said was true, it didn't matter how far they ran or how long they waited. At some point, they would have to accept that society as they knew it was gone.

He nodded toward the controls. "Let's try a few more. It's pitch black out now. We might get lucky and find some broadcasts from the East Coast."

Tucker slipped his hand out of Brianna's and turned back around. After fidgeting with the knob for a few minutes, he landed on a promising voice.

"Again this is Sergeant Lee Branson, I'm a 25Q with the 63rd ESB out of Fort Stewart."

Walter interjected. "Fort Stewart's in Georgia."

The three kids leaned in to listen.

"I'm broadcasting on a modified HCLOS radio

hooked up to my Humvee. I don't know how long I can broadcast before they find me and bring me back, but I swore an oath when I enlisted to support and defend the Constitution of the United States against all enemies, foreign and domestic, and I'm aiming to uphold that oath to the best of my ability."

Walter gripped the back of the chair, his knuckles turning white from the force.

"I've talked to my superiors, they've talked to theirs, and everywhere in the Army, the story is the same. The United States as we know it is gone. Without power, the government has already fallen apart. Members of the House and Senate fled their posts, concerned more about their families than their constituents. The president is alive, but completely ineffective. He refused to implement martial law for the first week, insisting all of the scientists were wrong and that the power could be resorted in short order. He said even if it was a lie, we should tell people not to worry, that it would come back on any day."

The sergeant exhaled in disgust. "How can I look a woman and her children in the eye and lie to her? I'd be sending her to her death. It might not be today or tomorrow, but every day she waits to get food and water is a day she doesn't have."

The radio crackled and Tucker fiddled with the knob, trying to keep the signal.

"Even the guys in my unit are leaving. All we have to eat are MREs. There's no way to pay anyone for their service. It's a mess. Fort Stewart is okay. All the base families have opened their homes to families living off base and they've developed a rationing system for the food and water stored onsite. The barricades have been closed and the whole place is on lockdown. But—"

The sergeant paused. "I just keep thinking about everyone else. The millions of Americans out there on their own with no food or water. I'm sitting up on this hill, broadcasting this message in hopes you hear me. No one is coming to help you. Get what you can, do what you can now, because this moment? It's the best chance you've got to survive."

The radio crackled again and Tucker turned the knob, trying to get the signal back. Walter stepped away, turning to face the windows of the radio booth. All of his worst fears were true. The blackout hit not just the West Coast, but all of the United States. For all they knew Canada and Mexico were equally powerless.

No help would be coming for the millions of people trapped inside major cities across the country. With little food and water and nowhere to go, how long could they live? How many millions would die over the next month? He thought about their meager supplies back at the house. Whatever they had would need to last as long as possible and soon, their strategy would need to change.

Walter turned back around and caught the wide eyes of his daughter in the light of the flashlights they'd propped up around the room. She smiled at him. "I guess you were right. It's nationwide."

"Seems that way."

He could tell from the way she held her expression

that Madison fought off a wave of tears. "What are we going to do?"

Walter rushed up and wrapped his arms around her. She might not be five years old and clinging to his leg, but Madison was still his daughter and she needed him. Maybe now more than ever. He ran his hand through her tangled hair. "We're going back to the house, getting you cleaned up, and then we can talk to your mother."

"I mean the future, Dad. What are we going to do? How are we going to survive?"

He planted a kiss on Madison's head before pulling back. "One day at a time." Walter glanced up and cleared his throat. "Who's ready to get out of here?"

Brianna and Tucker both raised their hands.

"Good. Everyone grab a flashlight and let's go."

Tucker stopped him. "Can we grab some of this gear too? I think I can make a portable radio that will work with a car battery. It'll give us a chance to listen to any more news out there."

Walter nodded. "All right. Brianna, you're in charge of weapons. Madison, you take the lights. Tucker and I will gather up anything useful here."

Everyone set to work and in minutes, they were walking out of the communications building and into the dark.

DAY TEN

CHAPTER FOURTEEN

TRACY

863 Dewberry Lane, Chico, CA
7:00 a.m.

"We're already at capacity. The back of the Jetta is scraping against every speed bump we cross, and the Jeep has so much gear tied to the top, it could topple over in a strong enough wind."

"We can pack tighter." Walter wrapped his fingers around Tracy's arm and pulled her close. Even in the dim light of the pantry, his eyes still held so much warmth and love. "You heard the broadcasts, hon. We have to take as much as we can."

Tracy exhaled. Everything her husband said was true, but she didn't see how they could take any more. When they walked in late the night before, Tucker set to work. He rigged up the car battery Walter had pulled from his rental car and the radio components they took from the campus building.

Within an hour, Tracy was listening to voices from across the country delving into their worst fears and bitter memories. Heartbreak and hunger awaited so many over the next few weeks.

She should have slept and regrouped in the morning, but Tracy couldn't shut her eyes. Every time she tried, her eyelids popped back open and visions of her wounded daughter with a shotgun in her hands filled her mind.

She got up and started an inventory.

Thanks to the house they had co-opted as their own, Tracy guessed they had enough food to survive four more weeks. Liquid would be tight, but they could make it last by using the juice and water from any canned goods and reducing showers to wet wipe downs and braided hair.

They could stay at the little house a few more days, eat the bulky food that didn't travel or store well, and then take what remained on the road. Peyton and Drew were in no condition to travel anyway. Although Peyton could carry on a conversation, he still suffered the lingering effects of the concussion. And Drew couldn't speak more than a sentence before exhausting himself.

Time was such a double-edged sword now. On the one hand, every day they spent in one place meant another opportunity to forage and plan and make their long-term supplies last. But it also meant more risk. The street outside might be quiet now, but it wouldn't be forever.

People would find them and they would have to fight.

Again.

She leaned into her husband's embrace and closed her eyes. "We need a few days, Walter. Drew and Peyton are still too weak to travel. Maybe if we scout around, we can find a bigger car. Then we can take more."

Walter ran his hand up and down her back, soothing away the tension. "Have I told you lately how much you mean to me?"

Tracy pulled back and searched her husband's face. "We haven't had a lot of time to think, let alone talk."

"I know. And that needs to change. Now that we know more about… the future… we need to start acting accordingly."

"What are you saying?"

Her husband smiled, eyes wandering over her face as he tucked a strand of hair behind her ear. "This isn't a temporary hardship. We're not on a race course just trying to make it to the end." He paused. "There is no end. It's only this."

"You mean this is as good as it's going to get." A furry nudge against Tracy's leg made her start. She bent down and Fireball mewled as she scooped him up. Cats always had a way of showing up to prove a point.

Walter reached out and ran a hand through his fur. "We need to make the most of every moment. Ever since the power went out, I've been on a mission. Whether it's landing a plane in the dark or getting back to you or heading to Truckee, I haven't stopped to slow down for more than a half an hour."

Tracy raised an eyebrow. Her husband had always been the on-the-go type. Even when they took a vacation to unplug and recharge, he couldn't sit next to her in a beach chair and watch the tide roll in. He needed to be up with the sun, hiking and exploring and seeing somewhere new. The end of the world couldn't have changed him that much.

"I can't believe you want to slow down. That's not the Walter I know."

He shook his head. "Not slow down, but..." He glanced at the pantry shelves as he tried to put his thoughts into words. "Prioritize. It's like the saying we used to throw around in the Corps. Slow is smooth and smooth is fast."

Tracy thought the words over. It reminded her of Girl Scouts and how so many skills took careful practice to gain proficiency. Rushing through a sewing project or an archery lesson only resulted in loose stitches and missed targets.

She nodded. "We need to stop running and think through our next steps."

"Exactly. I don't want to leave here until we've exhausted everything Chico has to offer."

"Then we should go to the Agricultural Department."

Tracy turned around to see their daughter standing in the doorway. With the sun from the kitchen windows backlighting the space, Madison looked more like a shadowy ghost than a live teenager. But her words carried real weight.

"Brianna told me about it when we were waiting for

you in the communications building, Dad. She says it's almost as big as UC Davis. That means seeds and plants and fertilizer and maybe even livestock."

"We don't have a trailer to haul any pigs or cows anywhere, Madison."

"The Ag department must. Animals mean food. Survival. After what we heard last night, we need to think long-term."

Tracy let go of her husband and smiled. "She's definitely your daughter."

"Indeed." Walter held out his hand and Madison walked up to him as she placed her palm on top of his. "And I wouldn't have it any other way."

"*Ugh.* Since when did the pantry become the hot spot for family bonding time?" Brianna walked into the small space, scrunching up her nose as she slipped past Tracy to survey the supplies.

The Sloane family broke apart after a quick hug. Walter disappeared into the kitchen and Tracy turned to Brianna. It had to be difficult to watch the three of them together when Brianna's family could be a hundred miles away worried sick. "I'm sorry it's taken so long to get to Truckee."

Brianna nodded but didn't make eye contact, focusing instead on the bag of flour in front of her. "Thanks."

"Madison mentioned you two talked last night?"

The twenty-year-old nodded again, but didn't speak. Brianna was so tough and composed in a crisis it was easy to forget she was less than half Tracy's age.

"Do you mind staying here a few days so we can load up on supplies and maybe find a new vehicle?"

"No. I don't mind. It's the right call. The more we can bring up to my parents' place, the better. The property is big enough for livestock, and there's a portion that's easy to clear, but my parents probably didn't think that far ahead. Getting there was always the first priority, you know?"

She shot a quick glance at Tracy and then turned back to the shelves. The quiver in her cheek expressed more than her words ever could. Brianna was worried and homesick and probably exhausted.

Tracy gave her a quick pat on the shoulder. "If you ever need to talk, I'm here, okay?"

Brianna nodded.

"I'll leave you two to figure out breakfast. Pick something that won't keep long. Anything we won't want to pack in a vehicle." Tracy turned to leave when her daughter caught her arm.

Madison mouthed the words "thank you," and Tracy smiled before leaving the little room. The more time she spent with Madison's friends, the more they became family. She couldn't bear the thought of Brianna hurting on her own.

Tracy walked through the kitchen and on into the backyard of the little house. There wasn't more than a scrap of brown grass in the back between the fence line and the little one-car drive, but Tucker sat out in the middle of it with a hunk of electronics in his lap.

"What are you doing now?"

He glanced up, squinting to avoid the morning sun.

"Charging solar panels, stripping some electrical wire, and seeing if I can't convert this radio to run on my little backup battery. It sure would be easier than lugging a car battery around."

"Any more news?"

Tucker shook his head. "The reception dropped way down as soon as the sun came out. I haven't picked up a single signal this morning."

Tracy watched him work in silence, thinking over all the testimonies they heard the night before. So many people trapped in their own little worlds, speaking into the giant void of what used to be 24/7 noise.

"Have you noticed how much more sound there is now?"

Tucker paused and looked back up. "Don't you mean less?"

"No. I mean more. I've never heard so many birds or crickets or other little bugs and critters. I was standing out here this morning and the sound of a squirrel climbing up the tree caught my ear. I would never have heard his claws digging into the bark above the street noise before."

She stepped closer to Tucker and bent down into a crouch beside his gear. "The world is noisy and busy and going on just fine without us."

He glanced her way. "Do you think we'll make it?"

Tracy tilted her head. "Society as a whole will have to change. I'm sure millions will die if they haven't already. I can't imagine cities being sustainable now. But the people who know how to farm and can protect their own little plots of land will make it. They might even thrive."

Tucker bent his head and focused on the wire in his hands. "I know most people will die. I've come to accept that. What I meant was, will *we* make it? Do you really think we can get to Brianna's place in Truckee? And once we're there, can we survive?"

He glanced back up, his eyes so hopeful and bright in the morning light. Tracy wanted more than ever to lie, but she couldn't. Not anymore. So she told the truth. "Honestly, Tucker, I have no idea. But we have to try."

DAY ELEVEN

CHAPTER FIFTEEN

TRACY

AGRICULTURE DEPARTMENT, CSU CHICO
7:30 a.m.

TRACY, WALTER, MADISON, AND HER FRIENDS SPENT the entire previous day inventorying their supplies. Brianna and Tucker unpacked both cars while Tracy and Madison took the house apart and collected everything useful. Walter laid out all the first-aid supplies and medicine.

By the time the five of them finished, it was evening and everyone was spent. But it confirmed their worst fears. Without finding a way to grow and harvest their own food, survival would grow increasingly difficult. They might be able to make it through the first winter and even survive after most everyone around them perished, but after that?

At some point they would run out of places to

forage. Without a garden and a farm, they would never make it a year.

"Are you sure this is the only way in?"

Walter nodded. "The greenhouse is our best bet. It's got good natural light, easy sightlines around the tables, and it leads directly into the main building."

"From here it looks like most of the plants are still alive." Brianna handed her binoculars to Tracy.

As she brought them into focus, dark green splotches of leaves appeared behind the frosted greenhouse glass. She couldn't believe it. "Someone must be there. They wouldn't survive this long without water."

Walter nodded. "That's why we're going in hot. I don't want a repeat of the Comm building."

Tracy lowered the binoculars and frowned at her husband. "Whoever is in there could be an ally. You seriously want to shoot first and not even stop to assess the situation?"

"Madison almost died because we didn't."

Brianna spoke up. "Madison isn't here and I agree with Tracy. We shouldn't engage unless whoever is inside is an actual threat."

Walter rubbed a hand down his face. The man was beginning to look like a lumberjack with his inch-long beard and uncut hair. "It's too risky. I won't allow it."

"You don't get to make that call. This is a group effort, honey. At some point you're going to have to accept that."

He frowned. "Not today."

Tracy rolled her eyes. "I'm not giving up, just so you know."

"I'm not either."

"You two argue like an old married couple." Brianna unholstered a handgun and checked to make sure it was loaded. "Let's get this over with."

Tracy followed Brianna out from behind a grove of small trees. She turned back to her husband with a smile. "Coming?"

"Right behind you."

It didn't take more than five minutes to enter the greenhouse. The second the door opened, the smells of fertilizer and rich earth and growing plants hit Tracy's nose. The humidity stuck to her skin and thickened the air. As Walter let the door shut behind him, Tracy fought the urge to leave.

Walter pointed with the tip of his rifle. "Each of you take an aisle. We can clear the greenhouse faster."

Tracy eased over to the right, Brianna to the left, and Walter stayed in the wider middle. With her gun drawn and pointing down toward the floor, Tracy advanced. Every breath into her lungs felt a bit more like drowning. Suffocation from countless water droplets suspended in the air.

She wrapped her free hand around the base of the pistol and raised it a few degrees, willing the claustrophobia to subside. The greenhouse reminded her of her past, not because of the richness of the smell or the vibrant colors of the plants, but the closeness.

The oppressive heat and stifling fear.

Pushing the thoughts aside, she focused on the present. Nothing good ever came from her childhood memories.

"There's got to be hundreds of plants in here. We need Madison to come and tell us which ones to pick. With all this, I'm sure we could set up a mini-farm." Brianna slung her shotgun over her shoulder and began rooting through the plants, checking the names and pulling out ones for Madison to look over.

"We should clear the building first."

She shook her head. "There's no one here. And even if there is, I can't imagine an Agriculture student shooting us over a few tomatoes."

"Brianna." Walter's tone hit like a slap, sharp and insistent. "Clear the building."

She opened her mouth to retort when Tracy stepped in. "How about Brianna stays here and works on the plants while we clear the rest of the building? By the time we're done, she'll be done, too. It'll save time."

Walter's brows knit together, but he nodded. "Fine. I'll lead."

Tracy stayed a few steps back in her aisle while Walter approached the door to the rest of the Agricultural building. He reached for the handle as it swung open and almost hit him in the face.

A man carrying a six-pack of seedlings practically shrieked and almost lost the tray, bobbling it up and down and spilling dirt before he backed up.

"Hands up!" Walter trained the rifle on the man, waiting.

The man looked down at the plants in his hands and then back at Walter, hesitating.

"I said, hands up!"

At Walter's repeated shout, the man shoved his

hands up in the air, the plants going right along with them. The little leaves wobbled above his head as he stood there, shaking.

"Hon, he's not a threat."

Walter didn't lower the rifle. Tracy stepped closer, reaching out to touch her husband's arm. He flinched as her fingers found skin and the rifle bobbed.

The man with his hands up let out a little yelp and the plants jiggled harder. Tracy tried again.

"Honey, he's wearing a shirt that says *This is How I Roll* with a picture of a tractor on it. He's not looking to hurt us."

"Sh-she's right. I-I just like plants."

Walter leaned over and lined up the sight. "I didn't ask for your opinion."

The plant man yelped again.

"Mr. Sloane, come on, man. He's a graduate student or something. If it weren't for him, none of these plants would still be alive."

"Is that true?"

The man nodded. "Y-Yes. I'm all but dissertation. I just…I need to finish this data set or I can't write it. If I lose the plants, then my whole year is wasted. I'll have to start all over and I'll lose funding and then I'll have to take a leave of absence and go work for my cousin Larry in Waukegan and—"

"That's enough." Walter lifted his head and lowered the tip of the rifle about a foot. "How do I know you're telling the truth?"

The man looked down at his chest. "I've got my ID

right here." He pointed his chin at the pouch hanging around his neck.

Tracy reached out and flipped it over. "Steve Larcen, Graduate Student, Agriculture Department." She let it fall and stepped back.

"Do you have any weapons, Steve?"

He shook his head. "N-No, sir. Well, if you count the pruning shears, then maybe?"

"Guns, Steve. Do you have any guns?"

Steve shook his head back and forth fast enough to have whiplash. "No. No guns. They kind of scare me."

At last, Walter lowered his weapon and Tracy exhaled in relief.

"You can lower your arms."

"Thank you. The lactic acid was beginning to set in up there."

Tracy shook her head. "What are you doing here?"

Steve's brows tucked in. "Just what I said. Finishing up my dissertation research. I've got about a month left and then I can write it."

"But the power's out."

"I know. It's crazy, right? I've had it take a long time, but never like this."

Tracy glanced at Brianna, whose expression mirrored her own. "You know it's never coming back on, right?"

Steve shifted the plants to one hand and scratched at his head. "Chrissy said something like that when she left last week, but to be honest, I haven't been focused on anything but this building right here for a few weeks. This next phase of growth is critical for my theory."

"Which is?"

"That select cover crops work as well or better than fallow fields and herbicides to improve soil quality and reduce weeds. It's been a three-year labor of love, but this is the final test. If the plants that I've grown in soil where my cover crop grew are healthier and less weed-plagued than my control plants, then my theory is correct. It could revolutionize organic farming."

Brianna began asking Steve about his research and he spouted off a bunch of words that sounded more foreign language than agricultural. Tracy turned to her husband. "I'll stay here and keep an eye on them. You clear the rest of the building."

"I don't like leaving you alone with him."

"With the tractor-humor graduate student? Walt, he's fine and so am I. Check the rest of the building and come back. Maybe by then those two will have run out of things to say to each other."

Walter frowned. "All right. But stay vigilant."

Tracy nodded. "I will." She watched her husband leave through the door before turning back to Brianna and Steve. He might seem more teddy than grizzly at the moment, but Tracy knew looks could be deceiving. While her husband cleared the rest of the building, she would honor her word and keep a steady watch.

CHAPTER SIXTEEN

MADISON

Agriculture Department, CSU, Chico
10:00 a.m.

"I told you I should have come with you from the start." Madison leaned over a row of bright green plants, foraging among the leaves to find the plastic signs with the variety names written in neat print. "Then all of this would already be done."

Brianna lifted a pole bean plant from Madison's hands and placed it on the table of things to take. "You're lucky your dad even let you trade places with your mom. The way he stared down poor Steve, I thought he was going to shoot him."

Madison glanced up at her father as he leaned against the far wall of the greenhouse. "The graduate student? One look at him and it's obvious he's not dangerous."

"After the communications building, your dad seems to think everyone's a threat."

Madison puffed up her cheeks and blew out a stream of air. When her mom came back from the greenhouse and told her to go pick plants, she didn't mention anything about her father being this…intense. "He's really that shaken up?"

Brianna nodded.

Crap. Madison knew the incident in the radio building shook her father. He could barely look at her without emotion lining his face and pinching his brow. But he couldn't take what might have happened and turn it into something more. She survived.

If anything, her father should see how capable she had become. Instead, he wanted to wrap her in bubble wrap and hide her away. It would never work. Not now.

"Finding what you need?" Steve, the graduate student, entered the greenhouse with Madison's father close on his heels. Although he traded the rifle for a handgun, her dad still kept a weapon trained on the poor guy. At least Steve stopped shaking.

Madison smiled. "Are you sure you don't mind us taking a few?"

"Not at all. Like I said, none of the plants in that section are part of my thesis. I was watering mine, so I figured why not water them all, you know?"

"I found heirloom pole beans and peppers. Do you know if there are any tomatoes?"

"Heirloom only?" Steve scrunched up his face in thought. "I think so. Harriet was working on a research project with tomatoes and squash. Those would be over on the far row."

Madison made her way there and rummaged through the plants until she found the ones Steve mentioned. She pulled out three tomatoes and three squash.

As she handed the plants over to Brianna, her roommate raised an eyebrow. "Why heirloom? They don't look as big and healthy as the plants in the middle."

Steve spoke up. "All of my research plants are grocery-store varieties. They're hybrid plants whose parents were pollinated by hand. The tomatoes will be big and red and just what you expect in the grocery store. But if you save the seeds and try to grow them on your own next year, they probably won't turn out."

"Seriously?" Brianna glanced around at all the plants in the greenhouse. "Why would anyone grow plants with worthless seeds?"

"Because they produce the most attractive fruit. That's all that stores and consumers care about these days. Biggest, most colorful, best-looking." Madison ran her hands over the leaves of the closest plant as she talked. "Have you ever gone to the store and bought a big, red tomato only to cut into it at home and have it taste like nothing?"

Brianna nodded. "All the time."

"That's because those plants have been engineered to grow a ton of massive fruits all at once so the harvest is bigger."

Steve chimed in. "But when you load up a single

tomato plant with that much fruit, it diverts all its energy into ripening the fruit, not imparting flavor."

Brianna stared at the two of them with wide eyes. "So you're telling me all the plants corporate farms grow these days are engineered to look good? Like a massive beauty pageant for crops where they look pretty on the outside but what's underneath doesn't matter?"

Madison and Steve nodded.

"Unbelievable."

Madison agreed. "It's actually worse than that. A lot of the plants we buy to be backyard gardeners are the same. They're just like Steve's research plants. Many tomato plants sold at home improvement stores are grown to produce one year of beautiful fruit, but nothing more."

"Why would anyone buy those?"

"Because people don't take the time to dry seeds and plant from them the next year when they can just go to a big box store and buy an already started six-pack of plants for a few dollars."

Brianna looked around at all the plants in amazement. "So all of those tomatoes you slaved over and babied at school, those were one-time only plants?"

Madison nodded.

"Unbelievable."

"Tell me about it." Steve walked over and picked up a small plant. "This is one of the best tomatoes for Northern California right here. It's an Amish Paste tomato, sort of like a Roma, but it's hardy inland and is one of the last to harvest."

"I've never heard of it."

"No reason you would when Romas are everywhere and grown in a massive scale."

Madison could tell from the way Brianna's eyes wandered to take in all the plants, that she was a bit overwhelmed. Even people as prepared as Brianna didn't understand the nuances to gardening. Selecting varieties of seeds to grow was as important as picking the right soil and location.

Too much sun and irregular watering and tomatoes would crack in concentric circles around the top. When exposed to too-bright light and wet soil, the leaves would roll up from the bottom. The tomato fruit would lose the shade necessary to ripen and not sunburn.

And those were just tomatoes. With California producing over ninety-five percent of the tomatoes in the United States, it was the fruit all agriculture students in the state knew the most about, but it wasn't the only one their little party needed. They would need a whole variety of plants to survive on their own.

Winter and summer squash, beans, peas, potatoes. Even corn if they could manage to till enough land. But they couldn't take more than a few plants. What Madison really needed were good quality heirloom seeds. The more seeds she could bring with her, the better their chances of long-term farming.

She glanced up at Steve. "Any chance Chico State has an heirloom seed repository?"

Steve smiled. "It's not a repository per se, but we do have a research lab. It should have what you're looking for." He pointed toward the building. "First floor, suite 105."

"What about animals? There's a farm here, right?"

Steve turned to Brianna and nodded. "It's massive. Eight hundred acres, I think. But it's about five miles down the road. This is just the research greenhouse. The farm is a whole separate undertaking. They've got goats, sheep, cows, and a ton of pasture land and plants. A bunch of people work there full-time."

Stopping by the farm might be worth it, but with that many potential employees guarding the animals, the risk might be too high. Madison hesitated. A pair of dairy goats would give them milk year-round and a first line of defense from potential threats. Goats were as good as dogs for their watchdog skills.

She pointed toward the building as she smiled at Steve. "Can you show us the research lab? Last time we went exploring in a dark college building, it didn't go so well."

Brianna snorted beside her and dropped her voice so only Madison could hear. "Better keep an eye on your dad or he's liable to shoot your tour guide."

Madison glanced at her father. While she had been talking to Steve, her dad never took his eyes off the man, waiting and watching with his gun ready. Steve wasn't a threat, Madison knew. But someone inside the building might be. Her father cleared it, but that didn't mean it was empty.

At some point, they would have to talk. "Dad, can Steve show us where the research lab is? I'm sure he'd like to have you lead the way."

Steve managed a nod, his face growing red like a ripening tomato. "T-That would be great."

Madison's father jerked his head toward the door. "Then let's go. Tractor Boy, you come up by me. We'll do this together."

CHAPTER SEVENTEEN

WALTER

Agriculture Department, CSU, Chico
2:00 p.m.

Madison bent over a tray of seeds as the graduate student pulled down another tackle box full of them. Something about the kid rubbed Walter the wrong way. Maybe it was the beer belly or the ball cap on backwards or the way he had a habit of checking out his daughter's backside every time he thought Walter wasn't looking.

Whatever it was, Walter refused to give the guy any space. He'd kept a gun pointed on him the entire time he walked down the hall to the research lab. Even now with Madison almost forehead-to-forehead with the kid, Walter didn't let up.

All he could see was Madison in that hallway, blood oozing from a cut in her neck and a shotgun in her hands. He couldn't lock her up back at the house and keep her out of harm's way; she was the only one besides Peyton who could pick the best plants and seeds for survival. With Peyton still recovering, Walter didn't have a choice but to bring her to the greenhouse.

But he didn't have to like it.

"Are you two about done?"

His daughter glanced up with a smile. "Almost. There's two more boxes I'd like to go through."

Walter kept his frown to himself, busying himself with checking the hallway for the twenty-seventh time. As he peered around the open door, Brianna came into view, her gun drawn and eyes alert. The more Walter got to know Madison's roommate, the more she impressed him.

Her parents had done so much more to prepare her for this sort of world. Had he and Tracy been wrong to shelter Madison? Should they have been fortifying a bunker and teaching her how to siphon gas and start a fire with a battery and a paper clip?

Madison wasn't as bad off as so many kids these days. She could shoot everything from a handgun to a rifle and knew the basics of animal care and camping thanks to her days in both 4-H and Girl Scouts. And the plant knowledge… that surpassed anything and everything Walter and Tracy could impart by miles.

But she hadn't grown up anticipating this sort of future. They raised her to think good things of her fellow man and to hope for the best in all situations. Now Walter wished they'd been a bit more pessimistic.

He couldn't help but think she'd be better equipped if she had a bit of Brianna's cutthroat nature.

He paused. What if none of this ever happened? Madison would still be at college, back from spring break and attending classes full of optimistic peers. When she finished the semester, she would come home and complain about all the college kids who didn't know the difference between a cucumber and a zucchini and then she would go to work on a farm for the summer.

Her life had been easy. Carefree. She knew hard work, but it was in the confines of plenty and abundance. There was never a time she went to bed hungry or risked her life to listen to the radio.

"You look like someone just kicked your cat."

"I don't have a cat."

Brianna raised an eyebrow. "Fireball's not even a little bit yours?"

"Nope." Walter eased out of the doorway and stood beside Brianna, canvassing the empty hall. "How's the packing?"

"Terrible. We don't have enough room for even a quarter of what Madison wants to bring. Unless we start lashing some of us to the roof of the Jetta, we're going to have to leave some stuff behind."

"We can't leave anything behind!" Madison's voice called out from inside the research lab. "I've already pared it down to the bare minimum. Without everything on that table and the seeds I've selected in here, we can't produce enough crops to be fully self-sufficient."

Walter followed Brianna back into the research lab. She stopped a few feet away from Madison, her palms stuck to her hips. "We're out of space. Unless we find another vehicle, it's not possible."

Madison glanced at her father. "Then we need to find a bigger car."

"I've been looking. But there aren't a lot of vehicles around. With the power grid failing during spring break, the campus is a ghost town. Anyone who stayed behind has already loaded up and left." He focused on Tractor Boy. "Almost everyone, at least."

Against all odds, the pudgy graduate student surprised him. "The Ag department manager had a work truck. It's still out back if you want it."

Walter cocked his head to the side. "What's the catch?"

Steve rubbed the back of his neck. "No catch. The keys are in the maintenance locker by the back door. I don't know if it has any gas, but it's one of those four-door pickups with a full-size bed in the back."

Madison swung around to face Walter, her eyes huge and shining. "Dad! That's it! We can take the truck, load the back with all the plants and still have enough room for a couple goats and some chickens."

Walter held up his hand. "Slow down. We don't even—"

His daughter wasn't listening. She'd already turned back to Steve with a grin a mile wide. "Come with us. We're headed to Truckee to a place where we can all stay for a while."

"Hey! I didn't give you permission!"

Brianna crossed her arms and glared at Madison.

Oh, no. The last thing Walter needed was to break up a fight.

Madison twisted around to face her roommate, cheeks turning red. "Do you mind?"

Brianna didn't say a word. She just stood there, glowering.

"It's okay." Steve interrupted the standoff. "I can't go. I've got to finish up this research so I can write my thesis."

Everyone turned to stare at him, but Brianna broke the silence first. "You do know the University system is basically toast, right?"

He glanced around. "I've sort of put that together, yeah."

"And that most of your classmates and professors are never coming back?"

"That's probably true."

Madison shook her head. "So why are you sticking around to finish a thesis no one will ever read?"

"Because I have to." Steve leaned back on the counter and lifted his ball cap to wipe the sheen of sweat off his brow. "This degree is the only thing I've worked on for five years. Two years of classes, three years of research and it's all leading up to this moment. I'm not quitting."

"But there's no one to award you a degree."

Steve shrugged. "I consider finishing it to be close enough. I can't leave here all but dissertation." He glanced down at his hands and his voice dropped a few notches. "My father said I'd never get this far. He thought… plants were a silly waste of time. But he was wrong."

At last, he lifted his head. "I'm going to prove it."

Walter exhaled. He understood the need to follow through and finish something that had been the driving force for so long. It was partly why he'd stayed on the airplane that fateful day even when his gut told him to leave. And it was why they were all taking Brianna to her family's compound in Truckee.

Madison had embraced staying there long-term, but Walter and Tracy weren't sold on the idea. How could he invite himself to live at another family's house? He would get Brianna and Tucker to the cabin because he'd promised his daughter to do just that.

He scratched his growing beard. Maybe he wasn't all that different from the graduate student with the green thumb standing across from him. Walter spoke up. "You're really okay with us taking the truck?"

"I am."

"Then, thank you." Walter reached out his hand and Steve shook it. "I owe you an apology. I didn't trust you at first."

Brianna snorted. "Try ever."

Walter ignored her. "I'm sorry. When my daughter said you could be trusted, I should have listened to her."

"Yes, you should have." Madison crossed her arms, but the smile across her face lessened the comment's sting.

Maybe not everyone in this new world was bad. Steve had proven himself to have no agenda whatsoever. He freely offered plants and seeds and even a truck and expected nothing in return. They should do something for him.

He earned it.

"Is there anything we can do for you?"

Steve squinted as he stared at Walter. "What do you mean?"

"You've been so generous with your knowledge and time. We owe you. How can we pay you back?"

Steve smiled and his face brightened with youth and inexperience. "Do you think you could help me break into the vending machine in the staff kitchen? It's got a whole row of Ho Hos I've been dying to eat."

Walter laughed and a weight lifted from his shoulders. Out of all the things to ask for, Steve wanted a pack of Ho Hos. But Walter shouldn't judge. The end of the world did strange things to people; he knew that firsthand.

Some adapted and some didn't, but they all changed.

He glanced at his daughter and Brianna before turning back to Steve. "Yeah, I think we can manage that. Lead the way."

CHAPTER EIGHTEEN

TRACY

863 Dewberry Lane, Chico, CA
7:00 p.m.

"I'd forgotten how good these iced lemon pies taste." Peyton licked his fingers, drawing every last fleck of sugar into his mouth.

"I can't believe you like those things. The ingredient list is a million miles long and every entry is a chemical." Madison wrinkled her nose as she dumped a cup of flour into a bowl.

Peyton smoothed out the wrapper and jabbed his index finger at it. "Not true. The very first ingredient is water." His finger moved along the list, pausing every time he found a retort to Madison's complaint. "And it's got corn syrup and vegetable oil and sugar. And hey! It's even got lemon oil." He leaned back, triumphant in the dining room chair. "It's practically a delicacy."

Madison stuck out her tongue and Tracy laughed out loud. Watching the two of them tease each other was a welcome respite from the stress of hoping her husband and daughter would make it back home alive.

"Give it a few more weeks and I bet you'll be clamoring for your very own little fruit pie the second we come across one." Peyton held up the wrapper. "Pretty soon these will be the new currency."

"Peyton's right. We should be hoarding snack cakes. They never go bad and in a few months people will be desperate for a sugar rush." Brianna sat at the other end of the dining room table, two handguns disassembled in front of her.

She poured a bit of unused motor oil they found in the maintenance room of the agriculture department into a glass bowl and used it to clean and lubricate each part. "There's so many things we took for granted before that we won't be able to get going forward."

Pointing at the bowl, she continued. "Like gun oil. It's never something I thought about. Whenever I needed to clean a weapon, my dad just had a little bottle of quality stuff in with the gear. It was just there."

"But motor oil works?"

Brianna nodded. "As long as it's clean and synthetic, yeah. I'd prefer automatic transmission fluid, but we'd need to hit an automotive store to get it. You can use Vaseline for the side rails if you need some grease, too. But I couldn't find any upstairs."

Tracy shook her head. Watching a group of nineteen- and twenty-year-olds adapt to a world without power was incredible. Instead of moaning and whining and waiting for someone to come save them, they all pitched in and worked together to survive. Brianna with her knowledge of all things survival-related, Madison and Peyton with their plant and farming education, Tucker with his electronic and weather-related skills.

They each brought something different to the equation, but what mattered most was the contribution itself. No one sat around looking to someone else to save them. They were saving themselves.

Tracy opened a can of pumpkin and handed it to her daughter. Without eggs, the muffins needed something to bind them together. It might not be fall, but the smell of pumpkin in the oven would be a welcome change from the growing stink of unwashed bodies and outdoor pit toilets.

Every time Tracy fired up the gas oven, she marveled. She had to light it by hand, but that was easy. The fact the gas still ran surprised her. At some point it would stop and they would need to burn wood or propane if they could find it.

"What type of heat do your parents rely on up in Truckee, Brianna?"

The young woman smiled as she ran her motor oil covered fingers over a recoil spring. "We've got a wood-burning stove and a buried propane tank. There's enough propane to last for one full winter, but after that we'd need to switch to wood."

Tracy nodded. From everything Brianna said about her family's cabin, it would be the perfect place to start over after the collapse of the power grid. Tracy glanced through the kitchen window to where her husband crouched with Brianna's boyfriend.

The two were hunched over the radio Tucker made the day before. Every time Tracy brought up Brianna's invite to stay, Walter shot it down.

He didn't want to be someone else's burden or responsibility. With Drew and Peyton, they had five mouths to feed and bodies to keep warm. She tried to explain that they came with assets as well. Between Madison's agricultural knowledge and Walter's ability to fly a plane and defend the group, they were net positive.

Walter didn't agree.

Madison leaned closer as she stirred the batter. "They've been out there ever since we got back. Any idea what they're listening to?"

Tracy shook her head. "I assume it's the same types of broadcasts as before. Random people all over the country." She squinted at the darkening sky. "With the sun down, they should start picking up broadcasts from farther away."

Drew eased into a dining room chair next to Peyton, groaning as he sat down. "What's this I hear about a radio?"

"Good to see you up and about."

"Believe me, it feels good, too. If I spent one more minute on that sofa, I might have lost my mind."

Tracy answered Drew's question. "Tucker rigged a radio to a car battery and is picking up broadcasts from all over. There's quite a few people out there with the ability to broadcast, whether it's from battery or solar or even wind power."

Drew glanced around the room. "From the looks on all of your faces I'd say the news isn't that we're going to Disneyland."

Brianna snorted. "More like a haunted house starring the ghosts of America before it all fell apart."

"Ouch."

"It's the truth." She fit the slide back onto one of the handguns before racking it and setting it on the table. "You of all people should know that."

"Brianna!" Madison chastised her roommate, but Drew held up a hand.

"It's all right. She has a point. If losing Anne didn't put it in perspective, getting shot a block from my condo did."

Tracy spoke up. "I think we all are aware how much the country has changed in such a short span of time. What matters now is what we do going forward. After what you all heard on the radio, I don't hold out much hope for aid to reach the majority of needy people."

"Neither do I." Walter stepped in from the outside with Tucker following just behind.

"Any new info?"

Tucker's grim expression said yes.

Walter nodded. "It's complete chaos in D.C. Half of the embassies are burning, the White House is under heavily armed protection, and the local national guard is patrolling the streets. There's a dusk to dawn curfew, but that doesn't do much."

"All it did was give the bad guys a window of time to act." Tucker shook his head. "They've tried to deliver aid a bunch of times, but a riot always breaks out so the aid workers leave. The man on the radio just now said his family is starving, but there's nothing he can do. He's helpless."

Tracy closed her eyes. Everything was as bad as she feared. Worse. "What about the president?"

"No one really knows. If he is alive, he's not talking. No government official is out there saying anything."

"That's because they're too busy figuring out how to save their own skin. You better believe most of them are holed up somewhere in D.C. with hot rations and military guards and a bed to sleep in every night." Brianna rolled her eyes. "All while the rest of the city burns."

Madison exhaled. "We're lucky that we got out while we did. Chico isn't a small town, but with most of the campus empty, we aren't seeing the same problems here."

"It's nothing like the D.C. Metro." Brianna set down the reassembled gun. "There can't be more than a hundred thousand people here. D.C. has what, six million?"

Tucker answered. "Something like that."

"It's chaos there because there's millions of people who don't have basic life-preservation skills."

"You're selling people short."

Brianna raised an eyebrow at her boyfriend. "How many freshmen did you meet who couldn't do their own laundry or even make spaghetti? Your roommate didn't know how to boil water."

Drew half-coughed and half-laughed. "Even I can do that."

"Right?" Brianna shook her head as she spoke. "We've all gotten so used to living in our little self-sustaining bubbles that we've forgotten what it takes to make it on our own. Even if some of those people got out of the city and into the rural parts of Virginia, they wouldn't know what to do."

"She has a point." Peyton sat up in his chair. "Before this all happened, I'd never fired a gun. If it weren't for all of you, I wouldn't be here. I know how to grow crops and farm, but even if I managed to shoot a wild turkey or a deer, I wouldn't have the first clue what to do with it."

"Neither would I." Drew winced as he sat straighter in the chair. "Walter's carried my weight ever since we left the airplane. I'm the one who got us trapped in the middle of a riot, got shot, and made Walter drag my sorry ass out of there."

"I wouldn't have left you behind."

Drew smiled. "And for that I'll be forever grateful. I think we underestimate the willingness for people to learn. I might not have skills now, but I can adapt."

"The college probably has an excellent library." Tracy poured the muffin batter into a pan as she talked. "If we could find it, I could pull some books on food preservation and off-the-grid living. Even some books on solar power and hydroelectrics."

"Before we do any of that, we should go to the farm." Madison opened the oven while Tracy placed the muffin pan inside. "If what Steve said is true, there could be goats and chickens and feed. If we could find an animal trailer, we could even take a cow."

Tracy glanced at her husband. Her gut told her to stay away from the farm. If that many animals lived there, they wouldn't be the first people to think about pilfering a few. "It's too risky. There are probably people still working there and others who know about it. We could be walking into a battle we don't want to fight."

After a moment, Walter surprised her. "The agriculture department turned out to be a massive win for us. Maybe Madison is right. It doesn't hurt to do some reconnaissance. If it looks like trouble, we can steer clear."

"And if it doesn't?"

"Then we might be eating a hell of a lot more eggs."

DAY TWELVE

CHAPTER NINETEEN

MADISON

University Farm, CSU Chico
10:00 a.m.

Madison sat on her hands to contain her excitement as they pulled the truck into a secluded spot a few hundred yards from the entrance to the farm. Her father had gone on his own earlier in the morning to scope it out and found no sign of anyone on patrol or standing guard.

"Like I said this morning, I have no idea if any animals are even here. It looked like some had escaped through a portion of fence by the road. There were caution signs warning the fence was electrified, but without the grid, it obviously wasn't live."

Brianna nodded. "Lots of goat and sheep farmers use electrified fence to keep coyotes out and their herd in. Without it, they might have just clambered on through."

Madison chewed on her lower lip. There had to be at least a few stragglers who stayed behind. "I'm sure we can grab some chickens, if nothing else."

"That's assuming someone hasn't beat us to it." Her father put the binoculars up to his eyes and canvassed the area. "There's four main buildings. One appears to be an open-air barn that's more cover for the animals than anything. One might be for pigs, one is definitely chickens, and the other must be maintenance or farm equipment."

"Any vehicles or trailers?"

"Not that I've been able to see. But they could be housed in one of the buildings. I can't tell. We'll need to clear every one and the surrounding grounds. It won't be easy."

Tucker leaned forward from the back seat. "That's why there's more of us on this trip." He glanced at Peyton beside him. "Even the gimpy one can use a handgun."

"You try getting a two by four to the head and tell me how you feel."

Brianna twisted around. "Knock it off, the pair of you. We need to stay focused. This place is big and unwieldy. It'll be easy to miss someone."

Tucker turned serious. "If you're that worried, maybe we shouldn't go."

Brianna shook her head. "No, Madison is right. If we could come out of there with even a couple chickens, it could be the difference between surviving long-term and not."

Madison looked up at her father. "You still think it's a good idea, right?"

His eyes warmed and his face softened as he made eye contact. "I do." He shifted in his seat to face Brianna. "I know you've made the offer for us to come stay with you, but I can't show up in good conscience empty-handed. The more we bring with us, the better."

"I agree." Peyton slid forward in the back seat until he could touch Brianna's shoulder. "We can't mooch off you or your family. We should be bringing as much as possible. The plants and seeds and vehicles are a good start, but livestock would be better."

Brianna glanced down at her hands. "Don't put yourselves at risk because you feel like you owe me something. My offer stands whether you show up with a trailer full of goats or only the clothes on your back. My parents won't turn you away."

Madison gave Brianna's hand a squeeze. "Thanks, but my dad and Peyton are right. We'll get you there no matter what, but we aren't staying unless we have something to offer."

With a glance up at her dad who nodded his approval, Madison took a deep breath. Whatever happened at the farm, they would be leaving Chico soon. Peyton was almost one hundred percent and Drew was stable enough to hit the road. They needed to finish up at the little college town and get out before their luck turned.

She motioned toward the farm. "Are we ready?"

Her dad nodded. "Let's do this."

Brianna eased out of the truck from one door while Madison's father climbed out the other. The rest of them followed, being careful to make as little noise as possible.

"The bushes along the rear fence line give decent cover. We can get in on the west side where the fence is partially broken. From there, we'll split up and take one building each. Who wants to keep watch outside?"

Tucker volunteered. "I'll do it. I've got good peripheral vision."

"Are you sure?"

He smiled at his girlfriend. "Don't worry about me, Brianna. I can handle it."

She frowned as she looked him over. "All right. If you're sure." As Brianna leaned in to give him a hug, Madison couldn't help but hear her whispered words. "Just don't get shot, okay? I kind of want you to stick around."

Tucker kissed her on the cheek. "Don't worry. I'm not going anywhere."

Madison's father cleared her throat and Peyton stifled a laugh.

"If everyone's done making me uncomfortable, it's time to go."

"Sorry, Mr. Sloane."

Her father nodded at Tucker and turned toward the farm, making his way through the trees along the edge of the road and into the scrub brush along the side of the fallow field. Madison followed second, with Peyton and Brianna next and Tucker pulling up the rear.

Every ten yards or so, they would stop, survey the farm, and keep going. Her dad was right; most of the animals must have escaped. Madison didn't hear a single bleating cry or see a single tail swish away the flies.

As they eased under the stretched wire fence one by one, Madison hesitated. "Maybe we should go back."

"It's too late. We're already here."

She shook her head at Brianna. "Something's not right."

"It's just nerves." Peyton put his hand on the small of her back to guide her through the wires.

"Let's just get inside and we can regroup." Tucker slipped under the fence and her father followed. He was the only one not offering an opinion.

"You feel it too, don't you?"

He brought his finger to his lips as he stood up. "Head to the nearest building. We'll regroup behind the wall closest to the fence line. I'll take up the rear."

Madison watched Peyton, Brianna, and Tucker each set off for the building while her father stayed back, rifle drawn and eye on the sight. With her friends halfway across the open space, Madison took off, hustling to catch up.

Her father joined them a moment later. "I don't see anyone. It could be that we're spooked over nothing."

"Or a bunch of bad guys could be hiding just on the other side of this barn."

Her father nodded. "That is a possibility."

"Who would ambush us here? It makes no sense. Why wait until we're all the way inside?"

Madison checked to ensure the handgun she carried was loaded and ready to fire. For a moment she pined for the shotgun she'd used in the communications building, but her shoulder still hurt from the force of the discharge. The 9mm would have to do.

Her heart thudded too fast and Madison forced air into her lungs, holding it there until her pulse slowed. "Are we still splitting up?"

"Yes. If there are hostiles in the area, we'll be harder to hit if we're in different places."

Somehow the thought didn't give Madison any comfort. "All right. I'll take the open pole barn."

"I'll take the chicken house." Brianna brought her left hand down to wrap around her right as she held her pistol straight out in front of her.

"I guess that leaves the shed over there for me." Peyton looked uncomfortable as he held the shotgun in his hands, but at least the effects of the concussion seemed to be gone.

Madison's dad followed. "I'll search the large barn here. Tucker, can you sneak around front and keep an eye on all the main points of entry?"

"Yes, sir."

"Holler if you get into trouble."

"Will do."

Madison's father glanced at each of them in turn. "Good luck. Meet back here in ten minutes."

Without another word, Brianna and Peyton headed off to their respective assignments. Madison didn't make it a handful of steps before stopping to dry her palms on her jeans. Fear made her sweat like a linebacker in a bowl game.

Chickens. Goats. A trailer.

She tried to keep all the goals in mind as she walked, head on a perpetual swivel as she scanned the area in front and behind her. She approached the pole barn and squinted to see into the shadows.

A tractor with conditioning equipment sat in the middle, and beyond a hay baler and a smaller ride-on mower took up the bulk of the space. With growing season barely underway, Madison couldn't believe any of them saw much use the last few months. She ducked behind the largest machine as she entered the barn, gaining a bit of protection from the metal body.

So far, so good.

As Madison eased closer to the far edge, she froze.

"I'm telling you, there's five of them spread out like damn spiders in a jungle."

The muffled voice didn't come from one of her friends. Madison's heart kicked into overdrive, her blood whooshing through her veins so fast, the strangers must have heard the pounding.

"But they're kids. We handled a bunch of kids before and we can do it again."

"Damn college brats."

Madison could only distinguish two voices. She didn't know if they were outside the barn, on the other side of the equipment, or even closer. Part of her wanted to rush them both. Shoot first and ask questions later. But for all she knew, there could be ten men right around the corner just waiting for an excuse to fire.

She couldn't stay still and not warn her father and friends. Even if it meant exposing her location, she would have to try.

Madison swallowed down the spit clinging to the back of her tongue and took a step forward.

CHAPTER TWENTY

TRACY

863 Dewberry Lane, Chico, CA
12:00 p.m.

Fear grabbed ahold of Tracy's spine, its icy fingers slipping into space between her vertebrae. She shivered in the warm kitchen. "Something's wrong."

Drew chomped on a leftover muffin. "What are you talking about? These are perfect. Soft, but not squishy, moist but not wet."

"The farm. Something's gone wrong. I just know it." She gripped the edge of the sink and stared out at the Jetta in the driveway. The feeling wouldn't go away.

It was the same dread that shocked her into action when those two men showed up in George's apartment. On some level, she had known if she didn't act, if she didn't take charge and eliminate the threat right then, it would be over.

Her whole body trembled. Her family was in trouble. She could feel it.

Tracy spun around at the sound of a slide racking. Drew stood at the dining room table, handgun in his hand. He held it out to her with the barrel pointed toward the floor. "What are we waiting for? If you think something's wrong, we need to be there."

"You're too sick. You can't fight."

"Yes, I can. You all have been babying me for days. The antibiotic worked. The fever is gone, the wound is healing, and I'm up on my feet."

Tracy shook her head. "I can't ask you to come."

"You don't have a choice. I'm not going to sit here while you go off on your own. If they're in trouble, the more backup, the better."

The last thing Tracy wanted to do was put Drew in danger. The man almost died. He should be resting until the wound in his shoulder healed completely, not rushing off to fight a battle that might be all in her head.

He cracked a smile. "You can stare at me all you want and try to come up with a way to keep me here, or we can get in the car and help."

Tracy exhaled and let her head sag. Her husband went through hell to keep Drew alive. If she dragged him out into danger before he was ready…

But if Walter got hurt or one of the kids…

At last, Tracy took the gun with a nod. "Okay. Just don't do anything stupid."

Drew held up his hands. "Believe me, getting shot once is enough for me. I'm not looking for an encore."

"All right. Then let's go."

She grabbed the keys to the car, slipped the handgun into her waistband, and followed Drew out into the backyard. The bright midday sun hit her face, but still Tracy couldn't shake the cold that crept into her middle the second her husband and daughter left for the farm.

If anything, it grew stronger, fighting against the warmth of the sun to remind her of everything at stake. They shouldn't have gone. A farm was such an easy target.

Tracy's fingers shook as she tried to put the key in the ignition.

Drew reached out from the passenger seat and steadied her hand. "We'll get there in time."

"I hope you're right." Tracy revved the engine and eased down the driveway and onto the quiet road. They had been lucky in Chico. After the communications building, no one had bothered them. It had been too easy.

Too many hours had gone by where no one was trying to take what they had. Silence bred complacency and confidence. Tracy held onto the steering wheel so tight, her knuckles turned white.

They'll be all right.

The drive to the university farm only took minutes, but every one stretched for an hour in Tracy's mind. Visions of finding everyone dead consumed her. Would they be too late? Would they make it in time?

The curve in the road Walter described that morning came into view and Tracy looked for the truck. It wasn't there.

Oh, no.

Her tongue turned to brick and her throat to mortar. The words came out slow and thick. "The truck isn't there."

Drew leaned down to peer out the driver's side window. "Maybe they moved it." Drew twisted in the front seat, grunting as his shoulder pulled. "I don't see any sign of a struggle. There's no tire tracks or run-over bushes. It's been a few hours; they could have cleared the farm already and are hitching up a tractor."

"I don't think so."

Drew turned back around to face front. "So what's the plan?"

"I'm going to drive in there and get my family."

"Whoa. Don't you want to circle around and check it out before we just pull up in there?"

"Nope."

He fell back on the seat and closed his eyes. "You and Walter have got to be the craziest people I've ever met."

Tracy let out a snort. "We're not crazy, Drew. We just make the hard choices." She eased the car to the side of the road about twenty feet from the entrance to the farm. As she turned off the engine, she smiled at Drew. "Whatever happens, follow my lead."

CHAPTER TWENTY-ONE

WALTER

University Farm, CSU Chico
12:00 p.m.

"I never got a visual, but I only heard two voices."

"And you're sure they haven't seen me?"

"They think you're a college kid." Madison pointed at his ball cap. "The Chico State hat was a good call."

Walter nodded. As soon as they arrived, the artificial quiet pricked Walter's ears. No birds. No squirrels chittering on the roof. If the farm was abandoned, there would be something.

Instead, in every barn, down every path, quiet.

He checked his rifle and exhaled. He would need to confront whoever was there and deal with the situation, hopefully without bloodshed. "You find the others and regroup. I want you safe and well-hidden."

Madison's eyes went wide. "Dad! No! You can't go out there all by yourself."

"I won't. You'll be my cover. But we need to assess the threat. I'll make myself known and get a read on them. Maybe they're scared and trying to protect what they have."

His daughter shook her head. "No. I'm not agreeing to that. You could be walking into an ambush."

They had been so lucky at the greenhouse. Would it hold or would this be a repeat of the communications building? Walter handed the rifle over to his daughter. "Take this and go. I'll give you ten minutes. After that, I'm walking out."

Madison handed over her handgun and gripped the rifle with two hands. He could tell by the way her jaw set and her shoulders tensed that Madison hated his idea. But he couldn't risk her again. He might need her and the others to end this, but he would protect them as much as he could.

This wasn't about him being the hero or sheltering her as much as it was base instinct. He couldn't put his daughter in harm's way on purpose. He had to keep her alive. Madison stood in front of him a moment longer, frowning at the rifle before taking off for the nearest building.

So far, whomever she heard hadn't made it to this portion of the farm. Walter eased down to the opposite end of the building and glanced around the corner. *Clear*. He felt like a dog ready to flush out a flock of birds so the hunters on their horses could shoot.

Only he didn't know which hunters would do the shooting.

As Walter braced himself on the wall of the barn, his fingers rubbing against the faded red paint, a familiar voice pierced the silence.

"Hello? Is anyone here?"

No. Nononono. It can't be. Walter swallowed down a wave of panic.

"Our car just ran out of gas and we're hoping someone can help. Hello?"

Walter eased back toward the edge of the barn and stuck his head around the corner. His wife stood in between two buildings, hands cupped around her mouth as she shouted.

From his distance, he couldn't see a weapon anywhere on her body. *Damn it.*

Whatever Tracy thought she was doing, it wouldn't work. She was going to get herself killed.

"Hey there, pretty lady, how can I help you?"

A man appeared out of nowhere, hunting rifle hanging from a strap on his shoulder. His beard and scraggly hair obscured most of his face, but the tanned skin of his hands and forearms said farmer. The grease stains on his denim shirt were either from the farm equipment or a car that wouldn't start. Either way, he was used to hard, dirty work.

Not the type of person Walter wanted to confront. He'd take a greenhouse graduate student any day of the week over a man used to physical labor and difficult choices.

Walter wished he hadn't given Madison the rifle. If

he still had it, he could have taken the man out where he stood. With a 9mm in his palm, he couldn't do anything but wait.

His wife smiled at the man and Walter's insides twisted.

"Oh, thank you so much. My husband and I are trying to make it to Redding and our car just sputtered to a stop right at the fence out there." She turned and pointed, the motion accentuating the curve of her hips in her form-fitting jeans.

Walter didn't miss the man's gaze as it checked out his wife's figure. He ground his teeth together.

"Where's your husband now?"

Tracy turned back around with a smile. "At the car." She leaned in and her smile deepened. "He's not one for getting his shoes dirty."

The farmer chuckled. "City type?"

Tracy nodded. "I keep trying to tell him he needs to get out and get into nature, but his idea of roughing it is a hotel room with only a queen bed."

The man stepped closer to Tracy. "We have plenty of fuel, but it doesn't come cheap."

"I've got cash back at the car. I'm sure we could settle on a fair price."

The man's eyes roved up and down Tracy's body and Walter gripped his gun tighter. "Money's no good any more. But there's something else you could use as payment."

Something inside Walter snapped. He couldn't stand there a second longer and let his wife take this man's bait. As soon as she left his sight, who knows what would happen to her. A parade of horribles flashed across his mind's eye and Walter stepped into the clearing, gun drawn.

"Step away from her."

Tracy spun around, her eyes wide. She shook her head a fraction, trying to tell him to back off, but Walter ignored the gesture. He would take care of this problem.

"Who the hell are you?"

"Her husband."

The farmer looked up and down. "You don't strike me as the city type."

"I'm not. Now hand her the rifle or I'll put a bullet between your eyes."

"I'm afraid I can't do that."

Walter aimed. He couldn't waste anymore time. As he pulled the trigger, a shot rang out. The bullet pierced his dominant leg, midway between the hip joint and his knee. Walter jerked and his shot went wide as the lead tore through his quad and out through his hamstring.

Everything happened in slow motion after that. His wife ripped a small handgun from out of her bra and twisted toward the farmer. She fired without hesitation, one, two, three times. He clutched his heart as more gunfire rang out.

Walter staggered toward her, gun raised as the blood pumped from his leg wound to coat his pants. Tracy dove for the rifle, scrabbling on the ground for the strap. She tugged at it, unable to wrest the weapon out from under the weight of the dead man.

Another shot rang out and Walter turned to see Brianna with a shotgun in her hands.

No! It was all going so wrong. They were supposed to stay hidden and safe. Protected. Walter fell to one knee as he tried to find a target. Where were they? Where were the shots coming from?

His breathing slowed and his vision dimmed, but Walter sucked in a lungful of air and concentrated.

God, give me the strength to get through this.

He'd prayed more in the last two weeks than he'd prayed his entire adult life, but Walter wasn't going to stop now. *Just give me the strength. Please.*

He caught a flurry of movement to his right. "Over here!" He shouted for Brianna and the others to hear.

Another round of gunfire and Tracy screamed. *No!* She fell back, rifle in her hands, and brought it up to her shoulder.

Bang! Bang! Bang!

Again and again she pulled the trigger, firing in the direction of the incoming shots.

A shout filtered through the sound of gunfire.

Walter could barely keep his eyes open and he landed hard on his butt in the dirt. Before he could blink, a pair of arms reached up under his and began to pull him back. He blinked Peyton into focus. "No! Get back. You're going to get yourself killed."

Walter flailed, trying to push the kid away.

"You're not dying out here." Peyton dragged Walter behind a building and propped him up against the wall.

Something tight cinched around his leg and the world went dark.

CHAPTER TWENTY-TWO

MADISON

University Farm, CSU Chico
12:30 p.m.

What the hell happened? Madison frantically looked through the scope of the rifle, trying to find anyone to kill. The man who shot her father lay dead in a heap thanks to her mom, but there were others still out there, she could feel it.

Tucker crouched beside her, his handgun no match for the rifle Madison carried. "Is your dad all right?"

"I don't know."

Madison wanted more than anything to find him, but she couldn't. Not until it was safe. Her mom crouched behind a water barrel, gasping for breath but otherwise unharmed. How she'd managed to free the rifle and not get killed, Madison had no idea.

She shouted to her. "Mom!"

Her mother whipped her head around. "Madison! Are you all right?"

Madison nodded and pointed at the building across the open area. "There are more!"

Her mom nodded and turned back around, pulling up the rifle to peer through the scope. She brought it down and shook her head.

Nothing.

Madison's lungs ached with the need to scream. This had all gone so wrong so fast. She turned to Tucker. "I'm going out there."

"Not a chance. Your father already tried that and got himself shot."

As Madison started to move, Tucker grabbed her arm. "You're the best shot with the rifle. You need to stay here."

She cursed under her breath. He was right, but she couldn't stay there and do nothing. As she opened her mouth to argue, the sound of an engine revving cut her off.

Their truck barreled into the clearing, a man she'd never seen before behind the wheel. He hollered out the window. "Get in! We're movin' out!"

One by one a group of men poured out from various buildings like wolves converging on a kill. Madison counted six. As the first two reached the truck, her mom popped up from behind the water barrel and fired.

A man with a ball cap on backwards and one leg over the side of the pickup bed jerked and buckled. He fell back off the side. A volley of shots rang out from inside the cab of the truck and Madison raised her rifle. She fired, but her shot missed.

Again she shot, but the truck's wheels began to move, tires spinning in the dirt and coughing up dust. The driver had put it in neutral. With the dust screen giving them cover, she couldn't make out a clear shot.

They were going to get away. A horn sounded to their left and the Jetta appeared from out of nowhere, headed straight for the pickup. Drew sat behind the wheel, eyes focused on the side of the truck.

"He's going to hit it!"

Tucker jumped up. "He can't! There's a whole row of gas cans in the back!"

Madison shook her head. "What's that matter?"

"If he hits them and they burst or there's a spark anywhere, they'll explode. There's too much vapor in the cans!"

Before Madison could ask another question, Tucker took off, darting out from behind the half-open barn door, waving his arms and shouting.

The Jetta didn't slow. *Oh my God.* Madison raised the rifle. She didn't know what to do. She couldn't shoot Drew, but Tucker was headed straight for him.

Brianna busted out of her hiding space behind the harvester, shotgun blasting at the truck. Madison joined in, firing into the cab, trying to hit the driver.

With the dust and the movement of the truck, she couldn't get a clean shot. More shots rang out. Madison didn't know if they were from the truck, her mom, or somewhere else, but she kept firing.

Shouts and shots and confusion. The truck lurched

forward, heading for the exit and the road beyond. The Jetta followed, gaining speed as it entered the clearing.

A shot hit the windshield of the Jetta and the glass shattered.

"Drew!" Her mother stood up, rifle in one hand as she raced toward the car.

It slowed and her mom gained on it, reaching the driver's-side door as the car careened to a stop, front tires stuck in a drainage ditch. The truck peeled out of the farm and landed hard on the paved road, racing away as the dust in the middle of the buildings cleared.

"Tucker!" Brianna screamed and Madison spun around.

Oh, no. Please, no. She raced forward, stumbling to a stop at Brianna's side. Her roommate bent over Tucker as he lay sprawled out on the ground, blood coagulating in a pool around him as it mixed with all the dust. A bullet wound marred his chest and another ripped his pants at the thigh.

His eyes stared up at the sky, vacant and empty.

Tucker was dead.

Madison eased forward and reached for Brianna, but she shoved her away. "Get away from him!"

Brianna scooped her boyfriend up in her arms, cradling his lifeless form against her chest. Blood ran in a trail down his arm and off his fingertips and his head lolled as Brianna hoisted him up closer to her face.

Deep, throaty sobs echoed up from her roommate's chest and Madison ached for her. She wanted to help, support, do anything but stand there like a spectator on someone else's grief.

Where is everyone else? She spun in a circle, eyes landing on her mother wrestling with the driver's side door to the Jetta. Madison rushed over, adding her strength to the fight. Together they tore the door free and pushed it wide.

Drew sat slumped in the seat, head resting on the dash, floppy arms at his sides. Her mother reached inside the cab and felt for a pulse. After a moment, she pulled her hand away.

Madison exhaled. "Is he?"

Her mother nodded. "He's dead."

None of it seemed real. First Tucker, now Drew. That only left Peyton and her father. Madison grabbed her mother's shoulder. "We need to find Dad."

Her mother nodded. "He's with Peyton by the grain stores."

They took off together, her mom slowing as they passed Brianna still kneeling on the ground with Tucker in her arms. Her father sat up against the wall of a barn, a tourniquet on his leg and a grimace on his face.

"How is he?" She stared at Peyton, willing him to tell her good news.

"Looks like the bleeding is under control and he's regained consciousness, so that's good."

"I was only out for a minute. Pain can do that to a guy."

Madison kneeled beside her father. "Tucker and Drew are dead."

He tried to move, but fell back against the barn with a wince. "How about Brianna?"

"She's… with Tucker. Physically, she's fine."

He nodded. Madison's mother kneeled down beside him. "I'm sorry, Walter. I shouldn't have come. I should have—"

Her father silenced her with a finger to her lips. "Not now. We need to focus on getting back to the house. The rest can wait."

"What about Tucker and Drew?" Madison couldn't leave them there.

Peyton stood up. "Is the Jetta still drivable?"

Her mother answered. "I think so. It only stopped because Drew…"

Peyton nodded in understanding. "I'll get them into the Jetta. It won't be pretty, but I'll get them home. After I back it out of the ditch, let's get everyone loaded up."

Madison focused on her father. He'd been right to question coming here. Chico brought them more misery than anything. If they had stayed on course and driven straight to Truckee, Tucker and Drew would be alive. Her father wouldn't be shot.

They would be safe. Not ravaged and brutalized and exposed. Madison stood and wiped the dirt from her knees. "I'll go help Peyton. You stay here and rest."

Her father nodded. "Don't think I could go anywhere if I tried."

Madison turned in time to see Peyton kneeling next to Brianna, easing the burden of Tucker's dead body from her grasp. Whatever happened next, Madison wouldn't let those men get away with this. Somehow, some way, she would make them pay.

CHAPTER TWENTY-THREE

WALTER

863 Dewberry Lane, Chico, CA
8:00 p.m.

It took Peyton and Madison all afternoon to dig two graves. Walter hated watching his daughter lift shovelfuls of dirt over her shoulder beside her best friend. They shouldn't have been out in the heat of the day, preparing to bury their friend and his co-pilot.

Drew. A man he'd dragged through a riot and killed for to keep alive. He'd survived downtown Sacramento, the suicide of his fiancée, and an infected gunshot wound, all to die when he should have been right here, safe.

They had a plan. His wife and Drew were to stay behind. If they hadn't shown up… If they hadn't interfered…

"You're right to blame me. I'm the reason Drew and Tucker are dead."

Walter glanced up. His wife stood in the doorway, a dish towel in her hands. She twisted it as she leaned against the wood trim, her face stoic, expression void of emotion.

"I didn't say that."

"But you thought it. And you're right. We should have stayed here."

"Why did you come?"

She pushed off the doorway and made her way into the living room. "Something didn't feel right. I stood in the kitchen, staring out at the Jetta and I couldn't shake the sensation that you were all about to die."

"So you just showed up with no plan and blew it all up."

"Not exactly. When we got there, the truck was gone. It wasn't where you told me it would be. I panicked." Tracy eased herself down onto the coffee table, perching on the edge. "I thought we were too late."

Walter adjusted himself on the couch. Peyton's belt had done the job of a tourniquet out at the farm and by the time they made it back to the house, the major bleeding had stopped. Now his leg sat on a mountain of pillows, bandaged to stop any secondary bleeding. He'd taken the first dose of antibiotics from their reserve supply already to ward off an infection.

Unless something changed, he would survive.

He swallowed and asked the question he couldn't

shake. "Would you have gone off with that man if he'd asked you to?" The fear of her answer twisted his heart.

His wife exhaled and stared him straight in the eye. "If that's what it would have taken to ensure my family's survival, in a heartbeat."

Walter opened his mouth, but she put up her hand.

"Right then, I cared more about flushing them out and finding out where you were. Like I said, I thought we were too late. The truck was gone." She glanced down at the dish towel. "If you and Madison were already dead…"

Her voice cracked on the last word and Walter reached out to touch her hand. Tracy looked up through a curtain of unshed tears and the sight almost broke him. "I wouldn't have had anything to live for, Walter. You have to understand that."

He squeezed her hand, desperate to ease the pain etched into his wife's face. "I know exactly how you feel. When I saw you out there, talking with that man, something inside me broke. I couldn't let him touch you."

"I would have been fine. I had a gun."

"I didn't know." He let her hand go and rubbed his beard up and down in frustration. "If I hadn't rushed into the clearing… If I'd trusted you…"

Tracy reached up and stilled his hand. "You were trying to protect me."

"And I got two people killed. Tucker was just a kid for goodness' sake."

"He chose to run into the middle of it, Walt. Just like

Drew chose to drive the Jetta. You didn't tell them to do it. You didn't make those choices."

"But it's my responsibility." He pressed a fist to his heart. "They were my responsibility."

"No, Dad. That's where you're wrong." Madison stepped into the room, her jeans and shirt covered in dirt, smudge marks marring her beautiful face. "Ever since you found us on the road, you've been trying to shoulder all of the burden. But you can't. You have to rely on us, too."

"I don't want you to get hurt."

She smiled, but it was out of sadness. "You can't protect us. All you can do is help us to the best of your ability. Even as a pilot you're not on your own. There's a whole crew of people helping you keep that plane in the air and land it safely."

"That's not the same thing."

"You can't tell me that in the Marine Corps you didn't rely on others to do their job. You weren't out there on your own, trying to take down all the bad guys like Bruce Willis in a *Die Hard* movie."

"That's not what I was doing."

His daughter raised an eyebrow. "It wasn't?"

Walter exhaled. She had a point. But purposefully putting his wife and daughter in harm's way wasn't something Walter was sure he could ever do. "It's different when it's your job. Those men and women signed up to risk their lives. They aren't my flesh and blood." He reached for her and she stepped closer. "They aren't my daughter."

Madison bent down and wrapped her arms around

his neck. Walter breathed in the scent of her. Youth and innocence and the tang of hard work. His daughter was right. Without everyone pulling their own weight, they would never survive.

This wasn't a mission to complete or a plane to land. It was the future.

It was life.

She pulled back and he smiled. "I'm never going to give up trying to protect you."

"And I'm never going to stop proving I'm capable."

As Madison stood up, Peyton entered the room. He nodded at Walter. "If you think you can stand, everything's ready."

Walter eased his leg down to the floor. "If you can help me up, I'll make it."

Peyton rushed forward and slipped his shoulder underneath Walter's and wrapped his arm around his back. On a one-two count, Peyton lifted and Walter stood up. The room spun for a moment, the pain in his leg shooting straight to his toes, but he didn't pass out.

"Let's go."

Peyton started slow, easing around the coffee table one small step at a time. After what seemed like forever, they made it outside to the makeshift cemetery. Peyton eased Walter down into a plastic chair and stepped away.

A candle burned at the head of each grave, and every living member of their makeshift family held a light of some kind. Brianna stood by Tucker's grave, clutching his phone that still held a charge thanks to his solar panels. Her face was swollen and raw from crying and Walter wished there was some way they could comfort her.

But no words said over Tucker's grave would bring her boyfriend back.

Walter cleared his throat. "We're gathered here to celebrate the life of two men, Drew Jenkins and Tucker Eldrin. They gave their lives today as brave men, fighting to save all of us from death."

Brianna choked back a sob.

"Although we can't bring them back, we can honor their memories by remembering the joy they brought to our lives and those of everyone they touched."

"Drew might have had a hard time adjusting to this new world, but he did. Even after getting shot and losing Anne, he persevered. He dug down and found a way to survive. We are all thankful for the time we had with him and only wish it were longer."

As Walter finished, he said a small prayer and his wife and daughter joined in.

Brianna waited until they were finished to speak. "Tucker…" She paused, her voice trembling too much to carry in the night. "Tucker was the best thing that ever happened to me."

She kneeled down beside his grave, the light from his phone casting her face in a glow. "He loved me for who I was and didn't try to change a single thing. Even when I was being stubborn and irrational, he never blew me off."

Smiling through tears, she kept going. "This one time we were going kayaking in the river. He kept telling me the water levels were too low and we'd never make it, but I insisted." She wiped at her face and let out a small laugh. "We ended up carrying that stupid boat for three miles along the shore since the river was too shallow to paddle, but he never complained. Not once."

She paused and bent her head. "That was the day I knew I loved him."

Tracy reached for Walter's hand and squeezed, holding on as Brianna told more stories about the young man who had changed her life. Walter would have given anything in that moment to bring him back. But they couldn't change the past.

They could only keep moving forward. No matter the challenges or the obstacles in their way, they would keep going. Walter would get that girl to her parents' place in Truckee if it took his very last breath.

At last, Brianna turned off Tucker's phone and placed it at the head of his grave. She kissed her fingers and placed them on the screen before standing up. "I know you all planned to come with me to Truckee, and you're still welcome. But I can't leave here."

She wiped away another tear before wrapping her arms around her middle. "I'm going to track down the men responsible for Tucker's death and I'm going to kill them. One by one. They don't get to take the only good thing in my life away from me and keep breathing."

Walter nodded. He understood the need for vengeance. "Whatever we can do to help, you have it."

Brianna stepped back without another word and walked back into the house. Walter meant what he said. If she wanted to find those men, he would help. His leg might keep him from the front lines, but he could still fire a gun.

Peyton stepped over and helped him up. Together they walked back into the house. Walter turned and said goodnight to him, looking over Peyton's broad shoulder to find his daughter.

A chill rushed through Walter.

Madison wasn't there.

CHAPTER TWENTY-FOUR

MADISON

CHICO, CA
11:00 p.m.

MADISON CINCHED THE SMALL BACKPACK SHE CARRIED tighter to her back and eased between the bushes. Hearing Brianna talk about Tucker solidified the plan she had come up with while shoveling all that dirt. Back when she first met Brianna, one of the first stories she told was about her cousin's little Honda Civic.

While Casey had been at the movies one night, someone stole it. She had walked outside, ready to hop in it and make curfew when the parking spot was empty. It made Casey so mad that she spent the next week driving down every street in the neighborhood, searching for her car.

On the fifth day, she found it parked on the street. The steering column had been pried open and the car hot-wired, but other than that, it was fine. No damage. The police couldn't believe her determination, but Madison could.

Tucker died protecting their truck and everyone around them from a massive explosion. The least Madison could do was find it and get it back.

Thanks to the full moon and cloudless sky, Madison didn't need a flashlight. As long as she kept to the edges of the light, she could see well enough to get around and not trip over broken concrete or a stubborn tree root.

Based on her memory of the campus while they drove in circles looking for the student health center, Madison searched. She spread out in concentric rings, down one street and up the next, walking each one to the next block before turning the corner and doing it again. Over the next two hours, she circled the house ten times. A ten-block radius and no sign of the truck.

She knew it could take days to find them. For all she knew, they could be a hundred miles away or more. But Madison didn't think so. Thieves never fled as far as they should. Something about the arrogance of not getting caught the first time made their getaway weak and shallow.

Based on the way these men acted, they were local. That meant a house somewhere in town. If they worked on the farm, they were CSU employees. It would make sense they lived close.

The more she walked, the more Madison thought about everything that happened since she convinced her father to detour to Chico. The student health center and the communications building. The greenhouse and the farm.

Only one turned out to be safe. Was that what the future held? Seventy-five percent risk of death, twenty-five percent chance of a lucky break?

Madison frowned as she eased around a tipped-over trash can in the road. She could lie to herself or try to ease her conscience a million different ways, but the end was always the same. Tucker and Drew were dead because she insisted they come to Chico.

One radio broadcast and Madison uprooted a logical plan and threw their whole existence into chaos. Peyton got a concussion. She almost died. Her father got shot.

Drew and Tucker were buried a few feet underground never to see the light of day again.

She stopped in the middle of the road. Brianna was grieving the loss of her first love because Madison listened to her heart. She let her sense of pity and compassion for a stranger upstage her duty to her family and friends.

No more.

It didn't matter if she walked these roads for the next year. She would find the men who stole their truck. She would help Brianna avenge Tucker's death. She would atone.

Two hours later, a light in a front window caught her eye. Madison eased into the bushes beside a house a block away and waited. She had given up sticking to the dark after circle number ten without a single person sighted, opting instead to walk straight down the middle of the road. But now, she had reason to hide.

With every house she passed, her caution increased. Shining a light in a powerless world meant whoever sat inside that house possessed plenty of confidence and ammunition. Madison didn't want to find out how much.

It took over half an hour for Madison to navigate the front yards and shadows of the street. She stopped one house away, hidden behind a thick azalea and the front porch steps. The steady hum of a generator obliterated any chance of hearing the occupants. She exhaled in frustration.

Leaving while this close wasn't an option. With a deep breath, she snaked around the house next door, easing up onto the back porch on silent feet. As she stepped toward the rear door, the wood creaked beneath her foot and she bit back a curse.

If anyone stood outside on guard, they had to hear. She rushed to the door and tried the handle. *Unlocked.* She send up a silent thank you and opened the door.

As she shut it behind her, a light flashed against the glass. Madison ducked and held her breath.

"You hear that, Johnny?"

"Man, I can't hear nothin' apart from that damn machine Leroy's got runnin'. What's he need to waste all our gas for anyway? Ain't no poker game worth all that fuel."

"Don't say that where the boss can hear ya."

"Piss on him. I'm sick of sittin' around and doin' jack. That shoot-out at the farm was the most fun we've had in days and he wants us to lie low? We shoulda finished the job when we had the chance. Now he's got us chasin' down every last little noise like some dog after a rat."

Footsteps sounded on the porch and Madison rushed deeper into the house, crawling behind a couch as the flashlight beam tracked across the living room. Of all the houses and roads she could have searched, Madison couldn't believe her luck.

"We shoulda taken that sweet piece of ass when we had the chance. She woulda given us somethin' to do all right."

Madison swallowed down a wave of bile.

"Naw, man, she was old as shit. Now that feisty little blonde with all those curls? Hoo-wee, now that woulda been one buckin' bronco worth ridin'."

They were more vile and disgusting than she imagined. Not that it should have surprised her, but it did. Was this the future?

No. Bad people couldn't be the only ones left. They couldn't be the men to carry the American torch after the catastrophe.

The more the pair talked, the more Madison wanted to drop them where they stood. But she couldn't. Not until she cased the house out and found out exactly what they were up against. She stayed in a crouch behind the couch, waiting.

After a few minutes, the one on the porch called out. "Let's go, man. There ain't nothin' here but a waste of time."

His footsteps landed heavy on each stair and

Madison exhaled in relief. After counting to five hundred, she stood up. The flashlights and voices were long gone. She made her way through the darkened living room and up the stairs, careful to avoid the creaky middle.

Two bedrooms flanked the wall next to the lit-up house and Madison eased into the closest one, keeping low to the ground as she worked her way around the bed and up to the window. Still in a crouch, she rose up just enough to peer over the sill and into the house next door.

The upstairs was dark, but down below her, the windows were bright and wide open. A man sat in a chair at a kitchen table, holding playing cards in one hand and a beer in the other. He tossed a chip into the center.

A moment later, he slammed the cards down and even from upstairs with the generator humming, Madison heard his booming, menace-laced laugh. The boss, she figured.

Including him, she counted six. They had left two men dead back at the farm. She smiled knowing that had reduced their force. But still, six armed men without a conscience among them would be hard to beat.

They would need a plan of attack that everyone followed and would all need to act together. Madison stayed at the edge of the window, watching their movements until the light turned off, the generator went silent, and even the bad guys went to sleep.

She checked her watch. *Nearly four in the morning.* She

stood up and stretched, hoping no one still stood outside on watch.

With careful, measured steps she retraced her steps, pausing at the back door. *Here goes nothing.* She eased it open and waited. A shaky breath later and she stepped onto the porch. Ten steps and she touched grass. Twenty more and she was one house away.

Madison took off in a run. Weaving in and around bushes and abandoned cars and turned-over trash cans that smelled like death. She didn't slow down until she turned onto the street she now called home.

She took the stairs two at a time, unlocked the front door, and stepped into the living room.

"Thank God you're all right."

Madison jumped at the sound of her father's voice. "You're awake."

"Side effect of a bullet wound, I guess."

Madison shut the door and locked it. "Before you yell at me, hear me out. I found them. The men who attacked us at the farm. They're about a mile away, on the other side of campus. There's six of them from what I can see. All armed. One guy is in charge. He's a total jerk. The rest of them are too, actually."

She kept talking, rattling off everything she'd learned over the hours of keeping watch until her throat ached and she ran out of things to say. At last, she fell into a chair opposite her father and took a breath.

"Are you done?"

"Pretty much."

"Good. Because now you need to listen to me."

CHAPTER TWENTY-FIVE

WALTER

863 Dewberry Lane, Chico, CA
5:00 a.m.

Walter smiled at his daughter. Sometime in the wee hours of the morning while Walter sat in the dark, waiting for Madison to come home, it hit him. *My daughter's all grown up.*

It didn't mean that she wasn't his little girl or that she wouldn't always wrap her arms around him for a hug. But he had to stop treating her like a child. He knew she felt as responsible as he did for the deaths of Tucker and Drew. But instead of sitting around sulking about it and pining away over poor decisions, Madison did something about it.

She risked her life, *again*, for the good of the group. He still remembered all the firsts. The first time he took his hand off the back of her bike and she stayed upright, pedaling all the way down the block. The first time he said goodbye when she left for summer camp. The first date he'd terrified with a 1911 and a glass of scotch.

This was a new first. The first time he really saw the woman she had become. He swallowed, hard. "I'm proud of you, Madison."

His daughter blinked. "What?"

Walter smiled. "I'm proud of you. You almost died in a shootout, came home, dug two graves, and stood by your friend's side as she cried. You had to be bone-tired. But you didn't fall into bed and sleep away the terrible memories of yesterday. Instead, you went out there and took it upon yourself to help."

"I couldn't let Brianna down."

"She's lucky to have you as a friend."

Madison shook her head. "No, she's not. It's because of me that Tucker's dead. If I hadn't insisted we come here, they would already be in Truckee. All the things that happened here, they're all because of me."

Walther hated to hear her inner thoughts and all the blame she heaped on her young shoulders. "You're too hard on yourself."

"I'm not hard enough. I should have listened when Brianna told me to wise up. I should have thought the worst of people, not the best. Ever since the power went out, I've been trying to convince myself that nothing has really changed. That there are still good people out there."

"You're right. There are."

"Not enough." Madison shook her head. "Every time I've given someone the benefit of the doubt these last two weeks, one of us has gotten hurt."

"Tractor Boy didn't hurt us."

"No, but that was one time out of how many?"

Walter shrugged. He understood his daughter's train of thought, but he didn't want her to give in to it. She couldn't get run over by despair and pessimism. "Isn't it worth the risk to ensure we get those chances? That's why our justice system is the way it is; innocent until proven guilty. It would be better to have ten guilty men go free than one innocent be sentenced."

"The world is different now."

"Is it? How? Because life is harder?"

"In part."

"So because life is harder, it's okay to presume guilt? It's okay to shoot first and not bother to ask any questions?"

Madison frowned, her eyes searching his face as she tried to reconcile her thoughts and emotions. "Didn't you do that at the communications building and student health center?"

Walter shook his head. "No. Not in the way you're thinking. I assessed the situation, determined we were at risk—"

"You're splitting hairs."

Walter hesitated. "Maybe. But this isn't about me. I've lived twice as long as you, Madison. I don't want to see you so jaded so young."

Madison broke eye contact, staring at her hands in her lap before speaking. "If we keep giving people chances, one of these days, someone is going to take too much. You've already been shot. Mom burned her hand. Wanda, and Tucker, and Drew… They're gone."

She glanced up. "I'm afraid that one of these days I'll lose one of you."

Walter nodded. He understood that fear. It lived and breathed inside of him like a parasite, feeding off his life. "I'll be the first to admit I've done things these last two weeks…" He shook his head. "Hell, Madison, I've done things these last *two days* that I'm not proud of. But you're right, it's the fear spurring me on in those moments." Walter leaned closer to his daughter. "We can't live our lives constantly afraid the next person we talk to will put a bullet in our heads."

"Why not?"

"Because it's a life not worth living."

Madison leaned back and shook her head. "So are you saying we don't go after these guys? We don't make them pay for what they did to Tucker and Drew?"

Walter smiled. "No, honey. I'm not saying that at all." He tried to put into words the thoughts that crystalized in his mind as he sat awake through the night. "Once someone proves themselves to be untrustworthy, all bets are off. Those men killed without guilt or remorse. They took until we fought back. We can't let them get away with it or the next family who stumbles across them might not be so lucky."

During the stillness of the night when it was just him and his thoughts, Walter came to understand something about the world. It hadn't really changed at all.

There might not be a power grid to keep the masses

employed and fed and warm at night, but all of the trappings of life he took for granted were all superficial. Underneath it all, people hadn't changed.

Turning off the lights didn't turn off morality. The people who were content to cheat and steal now were the same people who ran stop signs and shoplifted and lied on their time sheets.

The only difference was the lack of enforcement. No supervisor stood beside the time clock, ensuring everyone punched in and out by the book. No guards stood beside the front doors to Walmart checking receipts as customers left. No police car sat at busy intersections, keeping drivers honest.

Walter knew what kind of man he was and what kind of woman his daughter had grown up to be. They would be challenged in this new world, but they wouldn't break. They wouldn't lose themselves in the dark.

"So you're saying you'll help me and Brianna fight? We'll go after those men?"

Walter nodded. "Yes. I may not be able to charge in, guns blazing, but I'll be there. We'll all be there."

Madison stood and walked over to her father before bending to kiss him on the cheek. "I'm going to make some coffee."

"You don't want to go to bed?"

She pinned him with a look. "No. I want to plan."

DAY THIRTEEN

CHAPTER TWENTY-SIX

TRACY

863 Dewberry Lane, Chico, CA
6:00 p.m.

"Are you sure we shouldn't take a few days to recuperate? Everyone's been through so much."

"You mean I've got a bullet hole in my leg, right?"

Tracy smiled at her husband. "Mostly that, yes."

Walter returned the smile. "I'll be fine. Besides, this is a team effort." He pointed at the sugar sitting on the counter. "Bring that outside, will you? Peyton is going to need it."

Tracy didn't know if the pain meds her husband popped that afternoon were turning his brain to scrambled eggs or if he really did mean the words coming out of his mouth. Walter Sloane was not a man to agree to team-anything except a game of pickup football or trivia night at the local pub.

But if he really meant it, then it warmed Tracy's heart. She grabbed the bag of sugar and followed her husband's slow limp out the back door to the driveway. Peyton stood in front of a gas grill with a pot full of something white and crystalline.

Walter took the sugar from Tracy and handed it to Peyton. "Make sure it's a sixty-forty ratio of stump remover to sugar."

Peyton measured and poured the sugar into the pot.

"Now turn on the heat and cook it slowly until it starts to melt, stirring the whole time. When it starts to look like peanut butter, pull it out, divide it up, and stick the rolled-up paper into it."

Tracy's eyes went wide. "What on earth are you two doing?"

Walter smiled. "You'll see."

Tracy took back the sugar with a shake of her head. Whatever it was, she didn't want to know. "Dinner's almost ready."

"We'll be there."

She headed back into the house and set the sugar on the counter before straining the pasta. A jar of spaghetti sauce on top and they had dinner. It was a far cry from what she usually made before the grid failed, but they were running low on food in the house. Soon they would either have to find another home to pillage or dip into the supplies they brought with them from Sacramento.

Part of her still hated rummaging through other people's things. What if they made it home and found their pantry empty? It could mean the difference between survival and starvation. But Tracy didn't know what else to do. If they decided to stay in Truckee, they could start a farm. Raise some animals and grow some crops.

They could become self-sufficient and no longer rely on the stores of others to keep going. Even if they didn't stay with Brianna's family forever, their food would last longer with two fewer mouths to feed.

It wasn't a happy thought. Tracy wished Tucker still sat next to her at the dining room table, joking with Madison about wacky science theories and explaining everything from radio waves to the earth's gravitational pull.

Even Drew had grown on her. In the moments when they were alone, he talked about his fiancée and how she loved to take walks through their downtown neighborhood and take photos of interesting architecture and street signs.

The more he shared memories of Anne, the more Tracy regretted not knowing her. From Drew's telling, she had a kind heart and an open mind. Her death was a preventable tragedy.

Tracy shoved the thoughts aside. Dwelling on their absence wouldn't help the current mission.

Everyone filed into the room right on time; the smell of dinner called them like kids to an ice cream truck. Tracy scooped heaping servings of dinner onto five plates and handed them out one by one.

Brianna took hers with a nod. The poor girl hadn't spoken a word all day, content to sit at the table and listen to Walter come up with a plan while she loaded the precious remaining ammunition into their available firearms.

Thanks to the shootout, they were down to the bare minimum. There would be no guns blazing and lighting up the night sky tonight.

Every bullet had to count.

After Tracy passed out all the plates, she sat down and picked up her glass. "To those of us who are no longer with us. Tonight we fight in their honor."

Everyone raised their glass, including Brianna, who snuffed back a wave of tears before taking a sip. They ate in silence, each one of them thinking over the events to come.

Someone would be hurt, no doubt. Tracy couldn't fathom going up against six armed men without some casualties. Her only hope was that at the end of it, the five of them would still be alive. She glanced at her husband. He seemed so strong and confident, but she saw the lines of pain etched across his forehead and the dark circles beneath his eyes.

As the sun set, Walter pushed back his chair. "Is everyone comfortable with the plan?"

Each person at the table nodded.

"Good. Then we leave in half an hour. Everyone take a few minutes to prepare. This won't be easy."

Tracy cleared the plates, focusing on the mundane task she could control, while Peyton ran quick warm-up sprints in the backyard. She watched him run up and down the driveway, jumping up at the end of each pass, his twenty-year-old energy limitless in comparison to her own.

Brianna slipped out the back and from Tracy's vantage point, she caught sight of her bent head at Tucker's grave. At some point, Brianna would need to take time to grieve. But Tracy understood the need to push on and the need to fight.

Walking away after Wanda died was understandable. They didn't know who attacked the house that night. It could have been Bill like the man they captured claimed, some other member of the neighborhood seeking to hide his identity, or a stranger. But this time was different. They knew who killed Tucker and Drew and had a plan to stop them from ever hurting someone again.

Tracy picked up the last glass and held it, emotions running strong inside her. Madison and her friends were so young. It pained Tracy to watch the last vestiges of their innocence die so quickly. She placed the glass on the counter and turned to face her husband. Walter sat at the table, wincing as he moved his wounded leg.

The man could barely stand, but he insisted on coming tonight. He'd taken so many pain pills, Tracy wasn't sure he'd even feel his wound opening back up. But if it got him through tonight, then so be it. They needed him.

I need him.

Tracy walked over and placed her hands on his shoulders. "Don't you die on me tonight, old man."

Walter chuckled and patted her on the hand. "Likewise." He twisted in his chair to face her. "I love you, Tracy."

"I love you, too, Walter." Tracy bent to kiss her

husband and lingered, her lips pressed against his until a throat clearing made her pull away.

Peyton stood in the dining room, awkward and scratching his head. "Everything's good to go."

Tracy smiled. "Thanks, Peyton."

"Want to help an old guy up?"

Peyton came over and helped Walter to stand. "You can sit this one out, Mr. Sloane, really you can."

"No. My actions were as much to blame for Tucker and Drew's death as anyone's. I need to be there."

"I understand." Peyton stepped back as Walter found his balance. He'd taken to using a cut down tree branch as a makeshift cane, propping himself up and taking the weight off his wounded leg. It didn't leave him open to shoot, but once Walter got in position, he could fire a rifle.

At least that was the plan.

Tracy laced up her tennis shoes and checked the shotgun one more time. They would be approaching in two waves, Brianna and Madison in the lead with small caliber-handguns. Not the most lethal of weapons, but the quietest in their arsenal.

Walter hoped with the hum of the generator, they could pick off any outside sentries before anyone inside even knew. The longer they could stay a secret, the better. Tracy and Peyton would follow with shotguns from the front. It was as good a plan as any, but still fraught with peril.

With one final check of gear and weapons, everyone piled into the windshield-less Jetta. Although Brianna's Jeep had four-wheel drive, hiding a canary-yellow vehicle wasn't the easiest feat. They needed stealth over maneuverability.

Peyton started the car and eased down the driveway, lights off. In the glow of the moon he could see just far enough to not hit anything major. As he coasted at five miles an hour, Tracy's heart tried to keep up, pounding the rhythm to the tires as they rolled over the asphalt.

Every block closer, her fear intensified, thrumming in her veins and jumping her fingers across the stock of her gun. She reminded herself why they were there in that moment: Tucker and Drew and the truck.

Those were obvious. But then there were the unknowns: a weapons cache and another vehicle. Any animals still left at the farm. Food. Supplies. All the things stolen and looted by the men they aimed to kill.

Peyton coasted the car into a driveway one block southwest from the house. He turned it off and turned in the seat. "Everyone ready?"

"As ready as we'll ever be." Madison put her hand out in the middle and waited for everyone to add their own on top. "To Tucker and Drew."

Tracy waited for her daughter to exit the vehicle before following behind. Even with Walter's slow gait, they closed the distance between the car and the house in minutes. Whatever happened next would mean the difference between life and death.

She took up position behind the corner of a house two away. Madison and Brianna crept forward. Tracy prayed.

When the first shot rang out, she sucked in a breath and advanced.

CHAPTER TWENTY-SEVEN

MADISON

316 Rosemont Avenue, Chico, CA
8:00 p.m.

Brianna took out the first guard with a single shot to the head. He crumpled like a stretched-out Slinky, each section of his body collapsing in on itself. Another guard rushed from the front, alerted by the sound.

Brianna fired again. It hit him square in the chest but didn't take him down. She fired again and he sagged to his knees. He opened his mouth, trying to shout and Madison took aim.

He fell face-first into the dead grass before she got off a shot.

Three bullets down. Not enough to go.

Brianna motioned for her to come forward and Madison closed the distance between them. "I don't think they heard from inside or they would be rushing out here."

"Let's kill the generator and flush them out."

Brianna nodded and took up position beside the house, easing closer and closer to the portable generator sitting five feet from the back porch. As she bent to flip the switch, the back door swung open.

"Hey! What the hell do you think…wait a minute! Boss!" Madison fired. The shot went wide, lodging into the siding behind his head. She cursed and fired again as he staggered back.

The shot went high.

With a half-full magazine to begin with, Madison only had five rounds left.

As she took a deep breath and aimed again, a shot blasted out from the edge of the house behind her and the man fell to the ground. Madison turned. Her father leaned against the corner, rifle scope up to his eye.

He waved her back.

Madison fell into the shadows as another man appeared on the porch. Her father took him out with two shots to the chest.

Four men dead on the ground around her. Two still inside.

She knew it couldn't be this easy.

A volley of gunfire erupted from the window on the side of the first floor, shattering the glass in a million pieces and forcing Madison to fall to ground. She cowered in the weeds beside the house while her father returned fire.

She wished he would conserve his ammunition. If he

ran out, he would be unprotected and they would all be exposed.

While she low-crawled for the safety of the neighbor's porch, Peyton and her mom advanced from the front yard. Both held shotguns up and ready.

As soon as her mother spotted her, she called out. "Are you all right?"

Madison nodded. "There's two men left. I think they've barricaded themselves in the house."

Her mother turned to the window. "Then we'll have to flush them out."

Peyton stepped back to take cover and set his shotgun on the ground before pulling two orange blobs from his pockets. He lit a lighter and held it to two paper wicks. Before Madison could ask what on earth he was doing, Peyton lobbed the little rocks into the open window.

In an instant, the room filled with smoke.

She stared at him in shock. "You made smoke bombs?"

He nodded. "Your dad and I did. Here," he handed two more to Madison and the lighter. "Light them and throw them in from the other side. This should flush them out."

Madison did as he asked, lighting both wicks before sending the bombs flying into the house. They both landed with little thuds and even more smoke filled the first floor. It swept up the staircase, billowed around the ceiling and flooded the kitchen.

In no time, they heard shouts and coughing.

"Is it lethal?"

Peyton shook his head. "No. But it can make your throat burn and your eyes water. I just hope they think the house is on fire and come running out."

Madison hoped the same, but as the minutes ticked by, her optimism faded. The men weren't coming out.

Her mother took a deep breath and let it out through her mouth. "Looks like we'll have to go in after them."

She turned to Madison. "I love you, honey."

"I love you too, Mom."

Madison watched her mom climb in through the broken window with Peyton on her heels. Brianna followed behind him. From the distance, she couldn't see her father, but she knew he would keep watch from his perch, ready to shoot anyone who came outside.

With a deep breath, Madison eased her leg over the window sill and stepped into the house. Smoke still clouded the air, but with every second more and more dissipated into nothing.

The house was one of those newer, long and narrow types, with a craftsman front and two floors. The kitchen opened to the living and dining rooms and Madison's mother eased past the couch, gun trained on the space behind.

She shook her head. *Empty*.

In seconds they cleared the first floor. That left the upstairs. If it was anything like the house next door, Madison knew four bedrooms and just as many bathrooms waited. Without smoke to shield their entrance, clearing it would be difficult.

Add in the low ammunition and Madison had to

force her feet forward. Peyton and her mom took the lead, climbing the stairs one after the other, pausing at every opportunity. As soon as they reached the top landing, Peyton motioned Brianna and Madison forward.

He took up position at the corner of the hall to act as sentry and last line of defense. If anyone tried to escape, Peyton would shoot them.

Madison glanced up at Peyton as she passed. They had been through so much together in such a short time. She was thankful he came with her to Sacramento and now Chico and beyond. It would be lonely in this new world without him.

The light from the moon outside barely made it into the hall and Madison squinted to see. Ten steps ahead, her mother twisted the door handle on the first room. She pushed the door open, using it as a shield as she held her shotgun at the ready. Brianna followed right behind.

Madison headed toward the open master bedroom. It was her room to clear. With the light from the wide-open windows, she could see enough to tackle this room on her own. That had been the plan from the beginning. But it still shot a bolt of fear through her heart.

She could turn back and wait, but what if someone in there was hatching a plan? What if they made it past her and down the hall? Her mother and Brianna would be exposed and it would be her fault. No, Madison chose this part of the mission. She would see it through.

As she crept inside, she eased around a queen bed. It sat up high and memories of horror movies with the bad guy hiding underneath filled her mind. Madison kept to the shadows.

Her heart thudded, loud and fast, and her ears rang in the stillness. *Where are they?* She couldn't believe they would hide like rats and not come out and face them. After their big show at the farm and the attitude she witnessed the day before, they should be chomping at the bit to come do her in.

She raised her gun and advanced.

The second she stepped past the bed, she realized her mistake. The open double door didn't hit the wall as she'd assumed, but blocked the entrance to the bathroom instead. Plenty of space for someone to hide.

She spun around too late. The man hit her in the shoulder in an attempt to knock her gun free, but Madison had pulled it in tight to her chest as she entered the room. Her father had taught that a few days before. Always keep hold of your weapon.

He came at her again, fists flailing, and Madison backed up. Her breath came in jagged gasps and she fired, not really aiming, just pointing and shooting and trying not to panic. The shot went wide.

The man came at her again and she stumbled into the bed, banging her hip against the carved-wood footboard. A fist landed square on her midsection, knuckles slamming into her muscles and cracking ribs. All the air whooshed from her lungs.

She couldn't breathe.

The gun wobbled in her shaky hands as she pointed and fired again. The man stumbled, the white of his shirt blooming where the bullet hit his shoulder. Madison fired again.

He fell to his knees. Madison thought about Tucker and Drew and Wanda. When that first man broke into their house, she couldn't kill him. That was the job for police and judges and juries. The justice system.

Not a nineteen-year-old with a gun in her hand.

But standing there, watching this stranger grip his chest as blood pumped from his heart to coat his fingers, she understood. Her father was right. She was the same girl as two weeks ago. She still believed in right and wrong. Service and humility. Perseverance and courage.

But now there were no police. No lawyers. No jails.

Bad people didn't get locked up and fed three meals a day with enough free time to learn a foreign language and get a degree. The people who killed Mandy at the radio station and Wanda back home and this man who caused the deaths of Tucker and Drew...

They couldn't be the leaders of this new American frontier.

A series of shots rang out from down the hall as the man in front of her slumped to the ground, his face landing hard on the beige carpet. A trickle of blood seeped from his lips, staining the twisted fibers beneath him, and Madison stared at him as his eyes turned vacant and hollow.

She watched him die.

At last, she turned away and searched the rest of the room, confirming that it stood empty. As she stood in front of the dead man thinking it all over, Peyton busted into the room.

"Are you all right?"

She nodded, eyes never leaving the man in front of her. "You?"

"Yes. Your mom and Brianna took care of the other man. The house is clear."

"Good." Madison reached out and fished through the man's pockets, searching for anything of value. A pair of keys, a lighter, and a small silver horseshoe. She ran her fingers over the horseshoe's edges as she stood up. Luck might have served the man well before the power grid failed, but now, no amount of luck would see someone through.

Peyton reached for her, wrapping his arms around her until she winced.

"Watch the ribs."

"Sorry." He reached up and stroked her hair, starting at the top of her head and easing down to her shoulders before starting over. "When that shot went off, I thought maybe…"

Madison pulled back and searched Peyton's face. The sound of fear in his voice brought doubt crashing in. "We did the right thing, didn't we? Coming here and killing these men?"

His eyebrows dipped low, but Peyton nodded. "They took our truck and all of our gas. They killed two of our own. If we didn't stop them, they would do it to someone else. Besides, now we can go back to the farm and see if we can track down any animals."

Madison nodded and pulled away.

"Are you two all right?" Her mom stepped into the room, a smear of blood on her cheek.

"Yes." Peyton turned to face her. "Nice shooting in there, Mrs. Sloane."

"Thanks. If you're capable of helping, there's two bedrooms still to clear."

Peyton stepped away from Madison with a last squeeze of her arm.

As he left the room, her mother looked her over. "You sure you're okay?"

Madison nodded. "I will be."

"Good. Because I need you to help with Brianna."

Madison's eyes widened in alarm. "Is she?"

Her mom turned and motioned for her to follow. "Just come with me."

CHAPTER TWENTY-EIGHT

TRACY

316 Rosemont Avenue, Chico, CA
11:00 p.m.

Tracy hoisted the last dead man's legs up in the air while Peyton carried him under the arms. They took the stairs one at a time with a pause on each one, until they reached the second floor. With one more push, they made it to the master bedroom.

His body landed in a heap on top of the others and Tracy gripped her thighs as she sucked in a lungful of air. "Remind me next time we go on a killing spree to pick some lightweights."

"Not funny."

She wheezed in and out. "I'm not kidding."

Peyton walked past her and out to the second-floor landing. After a moment, Tracy joined him, shutting the doors to the bedroom on her way. The men they killed didn't deserve a burial, but Tracy couldn't leave them to rot all over the yard. It had been hard work hauling them up the stairs, but it was the right thing to do.

She glanced at Peyton. "You all right?"

He ran a hand through his hair. "To be honest, I don't know. I've never… This is the first time I…"

Tracy nodded. "I understand."

"Does it get any easier?" He looked down at her with wild, unfocused eyes. She wished they could rewind the last few days and make all of this a bad dream. But it wasn't. They stood at the top of the stairs in a stranger's house with six dead men locked in a room behind them. That was their new reality.

She wiped the sweat off her brow with the hem of her shirt. "Are you talking about killing a person? Does that get any easier?"

Peyton nodded.

"I hope not. If it does, then we've got bigger problems." Tracy tried to smile, but it came out in more of a grimace. "We didn't do this tonight because we enjoyed it, Peyton. We did it because we had to. They took our truck, our gas, some of our supplies. Without those things, we couldn't bring any of the plants to Brianna's cabin in Truckee." She paused and took a deep breath. "The Jetta doesn't have a windshield and it's covered in Drew's blood."

"We could have found another car."

"Even if we did, what's to say these men wouldn't come looking for us? They had to know they killed Tucker and Drew and they saw Walter get shot. They might have thought we were easy targets now."

She ran a hand through her hair and pushed the sweaty strands off her face. "If they didn't come after us, they could have hurt someone else. The next people who stopped at the farm might not escape at all."

Peyton shook his head with a frown. "But who says we're the right people to make that call? Why do we get to make that choice?"

Tracy grappled with the same issues. "We made the choice to attack them. We didn't know what the end result would be."

"So that makes it right?'

"No." She exhaled and waited until Peyton looked her in the eye. "But we need to find our moral footing in this new world. There are no judges or juries. No police to arrest someone who's broken the law or remind people why they shouldn't do it in the first place."

"I don't think that gives us the freedom to kill other people whenever it suits us."

"I agree. But we need to be prepared to make the tough choices. Walter could have killed Steve, but he didn't. Madison could have killed Bill or any number of people back home. All we can do is make the best call in the moment."

"How do you do that?"

Tracy shrugged. She didn't know the answer to that question. "I can't tell you how to do it. All I can say is that I ask myself, if this person stays alive, will my life be in danger? Will someone I love die? Could this person find me and hurt me? If the answer is yes, then…"

"Tonight happens."

She nodded. They could talk the issue in circles, but

it wouldn't make the answer any more clear. "Come help me load up on supplies. There's a ton of stuff downstairs."

Peyton followed her down the steps in silence. They were on shaky moral ground. Tracy knew that. In the deepest parts of her soul, she understood tonight was about more than a calculated risk assessment.

It was about vengeance. No judge would order those men to pay for their crimes. No warden in a jail would lock them up and take away their liberty. In Tracy's mind, it was up to people like their little group to keep and maintain some semblance of order.

But she couldn't tell Peyton that. He needed to find his own way in this world. He needed to make his own determination as to where the line fell and whether he could cross it.

All she could do was hope that in the moment, he made the right decision.

At the foot of the stairs she stopped and turned to him, holding her arms out for a hug. The big guy bent and wrapped his arms around her. She smiled against his cheek. "Thank you for coming with us, Peyton. You've always been like the son I've never had. I'm glad you're here."

He squeezed a bit harder and Tracy smiled.

"Thanks, Mrs. S." Peyton stood up and turned away before she could see his face. After a moment of throat clearing and eye rubbing, he turned back around. "So… what should we do now?"

A voice from the other room made them both turn around.

"First, you can join an old guy for a drink. Then you can help tear this house apart."

Walter sat in the dining room with a bottle of bourbon and a handful of glasses waiting on the table.

Peyton cocked his head. "You know I'm not twenty-one, right?"

Walter waved him off. "As far as I'm concerned, that law no longer exists. Anyone who has my back in a firefight can have a little sip of liquid courage."

Peyton half-laughed and walked over to the table before pulling out a chair. "I could have used this a few hours ago."

Tracy smiled and joined them at the table. "Better late than never."

CHAPTER TWENTY-NINE

MADISON

316 Rosemont Avenue, Chico, CA
11:30 p.m.

Madison stood a few feet away from Brianna, watching and waiting. Her former roommate sat curled up in a ball, holding Tucker's favorite shirt in her hands. Every time she rocked forward, she twisted, the shirt now as tight as coiled rope.

She must have brought the scrap of fabric with her on the fight. Something to hold onto while she fought to avenge him. A talisman. Madison pinched the bridge of her nose to stop any tears. She couldn't cry now. She needed to be Brianna's strength.

At last, Brianna sniffed back snot and spoke. "I thought… If only I killed them all… I would be better." She sobbed and twisted the shirt even tighter. "I thought if they were all dead, I would feel something other than this ache that won't go away."

With a half-cry, half-shout, she turned to look at Madison. "But it's all still there. All the hurt and pain and everything. Why is it all still there?" She blinked her wet lashes as more tears spilled down her cheeks. "I'm still just as broken."

Madison crouched down beside Brianna and reached for her, sliding her arms around her small, shaking form and holding tight. Watching the strongest woman Madison knew fall apart tore at her insides. Seeing Brianna in so much pain, knowing it came from the loss of such a wonderful person like Tucker, it almost broke Madison, too.

But she couldn't break down. Brianna needed her. "I don't know why it's all still there. I wish I did." Madison rubbed Brianna's back up and down while she sobbed.

After a few minutes, Madison pulled back. "But there's one thing I do know. Tucker wouldn't want this. He wouldn't want you to fall apart now."

Brianna looked down at the T-shirt still twisted in her hands.

"He knew how strong you are and how tough you could be. He would want you to still be that girl who can take on six bad guys and never back down." Madison paused. "He would want you to survive, Brianna."

The tears started up again, but this time Brianna brushed them away, anger taking the place of pain. "I knew this would happen." She stomped one boot-clad foot on the ground. "I knew that jerk would leave me. I just didn't think it would be so soon." As the last words came out, she broke down sobbing again, too overcome with emotions to do anything but cry.

Madison wished there was something she could do or say to help. She eased closer until their shoulders rubbed. She might not have the words to relieve any of the ache, but she could stay there. She could keep Brianna company in the dark.

They had been friends before all of this, but now Madison thought of Brianna as more of a sister. Reaching out, she took Brianna's hand. "Whatever happens, I'm here for you. You're as close to a sister as I'll ever have. Whatever you need, I'll be there. If it's a shoulder to cry on, or someone to go shooting with, or even a sidekick on a quest for neon nail polish, I'll be your girl."

Brianna smiled a bit through the tears. "Thank you, Madison."

"No, thank you. We would never have made it this far without you, Brianna. I owe you more than I can ever repay."

Brianna wiped at her face again. "Just stay alive, okay? That'll be payment enough."

Madison smiled and reached for another hug.

A knock sounded on the door and Madison pulled away to see her mom standing in the doorway.

"I hate to interrupt, but your father is insisting we all gather together for a toast."

Madison raised an eyebrow. "With what?"

"Bourbon."

"You can't be serious."

Her mom leaned back and glanced down the stairs.

"Oh, I'm serious. And if you don't hurry down there and get some, I can't guarantee Peyton and your dad will leave you any."

Brianna wiped at her face. "I'm sorry I'm such a mess."

Madison's mom *tsked* at her. "You're no such thing. All I see before me are two young women who underneath all their beauty have spines made of steel." She cocked her head toward the stairs. "Come on, they're waiting."

"Not for much longer!"

Peyton's voice echoed up the stairs and both Madison and Brianna found the strength to laugh.

CHAPTER THIRTY

WALTER

316 Rosemont Avenue, Chico, CA
11:30 p.m.

Walter poured a finger's worth of bourbon into five glasses Tracy found in the kitchen and Peyton passed them around the table. Once everyone had a glass, he raised his in a toast.

"The last two weeks have been some of the hardest of my life. But tonight, I'm thankful for those of you sharing this table." Walter paused and focused on Brianna. "Although some of us are no longer with us, their memory is still fresh in our minds and will forever be in our hearts."

He took a breath and glanced at his wife and daughter. "Tonight we drink to not just what we've survived, but what the future holds. It's up to us to make the most of it."

Walter raised his glass a little higher before bringing it to his lips. The amber liquid poured down his throat and he drained the glass before setting it on the table. He meant every word of that toast and a million more he didn't trust his voice to say. Losing Tucker and Drew was the last thing he wanted.

Watching his wife and daughter take life-threatening risks wasn't easy. But they survived. The five of them still sucked in the evening air and pumped blood through their veins. They would live another day.

Peyton took a sip next to him and launched into a coughing fit, gagging and hacking as he set the glass down. "Ugh. That stuff's foul. How do you drink it?"

"One sip at a time." Walter smiled. "You get used to it."

Peyton pushed his glass up the table. "No, thanks."

Madison set hers down with a grimace. "I don't know. It's not that bad. Kind of makes me feel all warm inside."

Tracy gave Walter an *oh, great* look and he shrugged. Madison earned her choice whether to drink or not. She'd grown up so much in such a short time. Or maybe, Walter thought, she'd already been there, he just hadn't been willing to see it.

The ambush that night had proven a few things to Walter, most important of all that teamwork meant the difference between life and death. No one tried to be the hero. No one broke protocol and got injured or killed. They all worked together to accomplish the mission.

They all survived.

He didn't know what the future would bring, but as

long they could count on each other, they would endure. Survive. Grow.

Brianna took another sip of the liquor and cleared her throat. "I want to thank all of you for coming here. You didn't have to fight these men. You could have decided to just pack up and leave, but you didn't."

She glanced up at Walter before turning to Madison. "You stayed out all night and scoured the town to find them. I can't thank you enough for that. If you hadn't found them, we wouldn't be sitting here. I would always be wondering where they were and beating myself up for not finding them myself."

Madison started to speak, but Brianna held up her hand as she turned to Walter. "Mr. Sloane, you took a bullet, but kept on fighting. And then you risked opening up your wound or worse to come here and fight again. I couldn't have done this without you, so thank you."

"It's the least we all could do, Brianna."

"No, it's not." She shook her head and looked around. "All of us made a choice to come here and end these men's lives. I know it was hard and ugly and maybe a little bit wrong, but Tucker deserved it. He—" She stuttered a bit on her words and took another sip of bourbon. She grimaced as she finished. "He deserved so much more than a bullet to the chest."

Pressure built behind Walter's eyes, but he willed his emotions back. In the short time he'd spent with Tucker, he had grown to appreciate not only the kid's intelligence, but his steadfast commitment to Brianna. The two seemed made for each other. To watch her suffer without him was painful and tragic.

He glanced up at his wife. Tracy's eyes shimmered with tears and as she turned from the weight of his stare, one spilled down her cheek.

Walter knew that a disaster of this scale, whether caused by a terrorist attack or the sun, would wreak havoc. But living it was a whole different beast. He poured more bourbon into his glass and downed it.

So many people would die in the next few weeks. So many were already dead. When winter hit the northern states, people would freeze by the millions. By spring so many who survived would starve. All this little ragtag group could do was ride out this apocalypse.

No amount of heroics or sacrifice would stop the loss of life on a grand scale. Cities would burn. Governments would fall apart. People they knew would die.

But in the end, Walter, Tracy, and the three kids sitting beside them would emerge to rebuild and start anew. It wouldn't be easy. Hell, it would be the hardest thing Walter had ever done. Harder than OCS or TBS, harder than watching his wife give birth to their daughter. Harder than accepting that Madison was all grown up.

In the coming weeks, this little family would be tested, but they would survive. They didn't have a choice.

He set the empty glass on the table and smiled. "How about we pack it up for the night and come back in the morning? We can dig through this place a lot easier in the daylight."

DAY FOURTEEN

CHAPTER THIRTY-ONE

MADISON

316 Rosemont Avenue, Chico, CA
8:00 a.m.

"Remind me never to drink bourbon with broken ribs." Madison hunched over the sink in the trashed house, trying to decide whether her breakfast needed to come back up.

"Really?" Brianna glanced up from the living room with raised brows. "I would think a few shots of bourbon would take care of the pain."

"It did last night. But now I've got a headache and I'm nauseous, and every time I bend over to hurl, my midsections hurts like a linebacker hit me full-speed."

Brianna started laughing, a little snicker at first, but the longer she looked at Madison in her bent over state, gripping the counter like a lifeline, she lost it. Huge, baying laughs came out of her little mouth and she landed in a heap on the couch as she dissolved in a fit.

Peyton walked in carrying an armload of fertilizer and froze. "What's going on?" He stared at Brianna as she convulsed and snorted. "Did she have some sort of psychotic break? Please tell me she's not delusional."

With a cough and mighty wallop on her chest, Brianna righted herself. "Not delusional. Just amused. Our good friend Madison has her first hangover."

Peyton glanced Madison's way. "From the bourbon? Gross. How could you drink enough of that stuff to be hungover?"

Madison shrugged, then winced when it hurt, sending Brianna into another fit of giggles. "It tasted fine last night."

"Well, that seals the deal for me. No liquor, ever." Peyton set the massive bag of fertilizer on the floor next to the other items they found.

So far, the house had been a boon of non-perishable food and water and most importantly, ammunition. Thanks to the gun-loving men they disposed of, they now had ten boxes of 5.56 and four of 9mm. No more shotgun shells, but beggars couldn't be choosers. Madison was thankful they found any at all. Add in the guns and knives they confiscated from around the place and they were finally prepared for another ambush.

She looked over the dining room table piled with everything from cans of tuna and baked beans to boxes of crackers and a case of warm beer. They didn't know who lived here before the men took over, but thanks to their membership to Costco, Madison found an entire bin full of batteries in all sizes and a massive pack of unopened toilet paper.

There were even clothes in the closets that fit most everyone, including jeans and T-shirts and some nice new socks. They decided the night before that anything in the house on Dewberry Lane and this one was fair game. But they wouldn't break into another residence unless they were desperate.

It was arbitrary and sort of silly, but Madison liked it. They weren't just roving and pillaging and stealing with abandon. They took what they could use from houses already compromised. They weren't adding to the destruction.

"Do you think we'll be able to find any goats?"

Madison glanced at Brianna leaning over the supplies on the table. "Maybe, why?"

"When I was a kid we had a neighbor with two little Nigerian Dwarf Goats. Combined, they produced a gallon of milk a day."

"You're kidding."

She shook her head. "Nope. They could never drink it all so I had all the fresh goat milk I wanted as a kid. My mom even made yogurt out of it."

Peyton scratched at his head. "How did it taste?"

Brianna laughed. "Kinda like grass, to be honest. But milk is milk and a little seventy-five-pound goat is easier to manage than a two-thousand-pound cow."

"Those little guys weigh seventy-five pounds?"

Brianna nodded. "We had a goat versus kid weight contest when I was nine. The goat won."

Madison laughed. She had spent her fair share of

time around pigs and cows and sheep for 4-H, but growing up next door to dairy goats had her beat. "Were they loud?"

"Oh yeah. Whenever it rained and they were stuck outside, the little one would start screaming and the big one would kick at the garage door. They were worse than dogs."

Peyton shook his head. "I will never understand how Los Angeles and Sacramento were part of the same state. The closest I ever got to a goat was the San Diego zoo."

The thought sobered Madison right up. "Do you ever think about your dad?"

Peyton exhaled. "Once in a while. But it's like I said before, there's nothing I can do. He kicked me out of the family. He doesn't want to see me and the barricades around LA would keep me out." He paused for a moment and his Adam's apple bobbed. "I made my choice when I stayed at college. You all are the only family I've got left."

Madison smiled. "You're right. We are family."

Her mom busted in the back door, struggling with a giant sack. "I found a twenty-five-pound bag of rice in the freezer out back."

Peyton rushed to help her and the two of them managed to set it on the table.

Her mom exhaled in relief. "The rest of the freezer was hazmat material, but the rice looks fine."

"Who puts rice in the freezer?"

Her mom shrugged. "Bunches of people. It's not a

bad idea to store bulk rice that way. It keeps the bugs out of it."

"Eww."

Madison nodded in agreement with Brianna. "Bugs are going to be more and more problematic, I bet. Without power, we won't have any freezers for a while."

"Not until we get farther north. It snows in the winter up in Truckee. We should be able to store any meat we kill outside from November to March."

Her mom set the sack on the table and wiped her forehead. "Are you sure your parents won't mind us showing up? I know we've been through this before, but I can't help but ask again."

Brianna nodded. "I know, but I mean it when I say they'll welcome you. After all you've done for me, they wouldn't have it any other way." She glanced at Madison and smiled. "And Madison's my roommate; they have to let her family in."

"What about me?" Peyton stood by the door, his lips thin with concern.

"No one with arms like yours gets turned away by the Clifton clan. My dad will take one look at you and calculate all the firewood you can chop in an hour. You won't be able to leave even if you wanted to."

Peyton exhaled in relief. "Chopping wood is one thing I'm good at." He glanced at his watch. "I'll go see what else I can find in the shed."

He disappeared and Madison turned to her mom. "I'll help you finish in the garage."

Brianna clambered off the couch and made her way into the kitchen. "What should I do?"

Madison's mom pointed to the shed. "How about you help Peyton? We've gone through the house. All that's left is the outside."

Brianna nodded and disappeared out the back door.

"You really think her family will be as accepting as she says?" Madison leaned against the counter and wrapped an arm around her ribs.

Her mom thought it over. "I wish I knew, but I've never met them. All I can say is, I wouldn't be so quick to invite a bunch of strangers in. Not if I had the kind of setup Brianna says they do."

Madison nodded. She felt the same way. "If they turn us away, what will we do?"

"Find somewhere else to settle down. There have to be some abandoned places up north of here. If we can't find a cabin or a house, we can find an RV and set it up somewhere remote. That could tide us over for the winter."

"Then what?"

Her mom turned to her with a smile. "Let's just take it one day at a time."

DAY FIFTEEN

CHAPTER THIRTY-TWO

TRACY

University Library, CSU Chico
9:00 a.m.

"They have books on everything from hydroelectric to solar to wind power. Even zero footprint living."

Madison held up a stack of books and Tracy smiled. "A university as big as this should have everything we need. I just wish they had kept a card catalog instead of converting everything to electronic records."

"Tell me about it. This hunt and peck is exhausting." Peyton pulled out a book and read the cover with a snort. "*Stock Market Investing For Dummies*. Don't think anyone will be needing that for a while."

"How about *101 Ways to Make Money on the Internet*?" Brianna held up another.

"There's always this one: *Get Rich or Drown Trying: A Guide to Deep-Sea Treasure-Hunting.*" Tracy shook her head. There were more books in that library that would never be helpful for anything more than a good laugh or a warm fire than she ever thought possible.

A few weeks ago, if anyone even mentioned the possibility of using the library as kindling, she would have gasped and called them barbaric. But now all these books would keep someone alive. "Let's bring a few to use as fire-starters."

"Mom!" Madison's mouth gaped open.

"She has a good point. Some of the older ones have good paper for burning."

Her daughter shook her head. "I can't believe you're talking about burning books."

Tracy exhaled. She understood the revulsion. It wasn't something she wanted to consider, but desperate times might call for desperate measures one day. "It would only be in an emergency."

Madison frowned at her mother and set the stack of books to take on the table. "If you're serious, then we're bringing ones I want to read." She stomped out of the nonfiction section and made her way across the floor.

"Where are you going?"

Madison called out without turning around. "Romance!"

Even Peyton laughed. "No way! I'm going to the thriller section. I'm not spending the rest of forever with nothing to read but chick books!"

"Don't knock them 'til you try them." Brianna

pushed one book back on the shelf before pulling out another. "Some of those romances are pretty good."

"You read them too?" Peyton stared at Brianna. "I don't believe it."

She shrugged. "I might have borrowed a few of Madison's this past year."

Tracy smiled so wide her cheeks hurt. Seeing the three of them back to their teasing selves lifted her spirits like nothing else could. "As soon as you all find what you want, we should go. We still need to hit the farm before we head out."

Brianna nodded. "We can meet you out at the truck if you like."

"Sounds like a plan." Tracy watched each of the kids head off to different directions of the library, all looking for the last of the written fiction to be found in these parts for a while.

Tracy turned in a circle, staring at the thousands of books lining the shelves. Printing presses and editors and graphic artists. Novelists and biographers and textbook writers. All gone. How long would it take for them to come back?

When would America be strong enough to rebuild? What would it look like when it did?

She shook her head and picked up the stack of reference books on the table. Whatever happened next, at least they would be prepared to survive it. She made her way out of the library and over to the truck.

Walter opened the passenger-side door and Tracy smiled. "Hey there, little mister. How are you today?"

She set the books down and reached out to pet Fireball on the head.

"I see how it is. The furball gets a smile and a scratch behind the ears and I get ignored."

Tracy grinned at her husband. "Not entirely." She leaned forward and kissed him, savoring the brush of his beard against her lips. "But you have to admit, he's a bit cuter than you."

Walter pretended to be offended. "What? You don't like the lumberjack look?"

"It's growing on me."

Walter's leg healed a little bit more each day. In not too long, he would be able to ditch the cane and walk on his own. She hoped he would regain full range of movement, but even if he didn't, he was still alive. That was what mattered.

The sound of chattering and laughing pricked Fireball's ears and he clambered over Walter's shoulder to look out the back.

"The kids are coming." Tracy patted Walter's good leg. "Scoot on over and give me some room. I'll let Peyton drive to the farm."

"Fine, but he's not driving all the way to Truckee. That kid can't miss a pothole to save his life."

Twenty minutes later, they all piled out of the truck and the Jeep and stood in the middle of the abandoned farm. The dead body of the man they killed still lay in the dirt, flies buzzing all around.

"You all are sure it's clear?" Walter stuck his head out the window and hollered at the rest of the group.

Tracy nodded. "We drove through three times and

Peyton and Madison scoped out the buildings. It's empty."

"Good." Walter leaned back, about to roll up the window and wait out their search, when the little cat jumped in front of his face. "Hey!"

He reached for the little cat, but the scrap of fur was too quick. Fireball darted away from the truck and disappeared into the closest barn. Tracy took off after him.

It was irrational and crazy, but that little cat meant more to her than Tracy could ever explain. She needed him. "Fireball! Fireball! Here kitty, kitty."

He mewled and she followed the sound, stopping in mid-stride when she rounded the corner of two bales of hay. Fireball stood in a crouch, ears flattened. He'd cornered three chickens in the back of the barn.

Tracy whooped in joy. "Guys! Over here!" She rushed in and scooped the little cat up with no more than a meow of protest as Madison and Peyton rushed inside. "Fireball found us some chickens!"

Madison laughed in delight. "I'll look for a crate to put them in."

"I'll take Fireball back to the truck." Tracy walked outside with the cat in her arms as Brianna busted out from the pasture beyond the fence.

The feisty blonde gripped her knees as she sucked in a breath. "There's two pygmy goats just out beyond the trees. If we can find some rope, we should be able to walk them back to the truck."

Tracy couldn't believe their luck. The site of so much confusion and pain was turning out to be a boon of resources. Chickens *and* goats. She glanced at the dead body no more than thirty feet away. She could smell his rotten flesh, but it didn't turn her stomach.

They had won. Despite being shot at and losing Tucker and Drew, the Sloanes, Brianna, and Peyton had survived. With any luck, they would be bringing plants and animals and a whole lot more to the Clifton family cabin.

She handed Fireball back to her husband with a smile. "Today is a good day."

He smiled back. "Tomorrow will be even better."

DAY SIXTEEN

CHAPTER THIRTY-THREE

MADISON

TRUCKEE, CA
4:30 p.m.

IT HAD TAKEN THEM AN ENTIRE DAY TO NAVIGATE THE back roads with two vehicles, two goats, three chickens, and a yowly cat, but they were finally in Truckee. Brianna led the way over bumpy dirt roads that wound higher and higher into the mountains toward her family's cabin.

Beautiful didn't begin to describe the tree-filled hills and grass-covered meadows. In the fall when the rains returned the entire place would be verdant and teeming with life. Even now with more brown patches than green, the birds chirped and the blades of grass bent in the wind. It was so far removed from the destroyed cities they left behind.

Madison reached forward and punched the controls on the dash, pulling up the CD player.

Her mother glanced over from the driver's seat. "What are you doing?"

"Checking something." Madison pushed a few buttons and music blasted from the speakers.

Her father laughed.

"What is it?" Madison thought she recognized the singer, but she'd never heard the song."

Her mother joined in with the chorus belting out the words.

"It's the Eagles. You have to have heard this."

Madison looked at the display on the dash. "'Love Will Keep Us Alive'? It sounds corny. When was it recorded?"

Her father shook his head. "Before you were born. And now I feel old."

Madison scrunched up her nose. "Sorry. But hey, I found us some music!"

"That you did. Turn it up, Tracy!"

Her mother turned up the volume and rolled down the front windows. Fireball scrambled down onto the floorboards to hide from the wind and Madison stuck her hand out the window. It had been a crazy few weeks, but for the first time since the power grid failed, Madison really felt alive. They had survived everything from shootouts to car crashes and everything in between.

Now they were a few minutes away from the start of a new chapter. Brianna's lights flashed ahead of them and she slowed the Jeep.

As she turned off the gravel road onto a dirt driveway, Peyton stuck his head out the window. "Is that the Eagles?"

"How do you know?"

"My dad helped sign them when they got back together in 1994. I hung out with them when I was really little." He smiled a bit. "I did tell you my dad had a nice pool."

Madison shook her head in wonder. Peyton was as nonchalant about his life before as he was about starting over way up here in the mountains.

Brianna hopped out of the Jeep and unlocked a metal gate, swinging it wide to accommodate the vehicles. She turned to Madison's truck and shouted. "Can you shut this after you get through?"

Madison nodded and waited until her mom drove through the gate in Brianna's wake to hop out and secure it closed. She turned and watched as Brianna drove straight down a small drive toward a little cabin at the end of the road.

She climbed in the cab as two people rushed out of the cabin and ran toward the Jeep. The brake lights flashed on, Brianna jumped out, and in seconds the little trio was all wrapped up with each other hugging and laughing.

Madison's mom drove the truck slowly down the driveway and parked it just behind the Jeep.

Brianna pulled away from the embrace and pointed at the truck and Peyton inside the Jeep, her face lit up like a kid on Christmas.

Madison turned to her mom. "I guess this is it."

Her mom nodded. "I guess so."

The cabin looked small at first, but the more Madison peered past the vehicles, the more she saw. Multiple chimneys and fenced-in areas of yard. Fruit trees all in a row along one side. Land perfect for a pasture and a greenhouse beyond.

She turned around in the truck and smiled at her dad. "Are you ready?"

Her father looked at her, eyes glassy as he smiled. "You first, honey."

Madison opened the door to the truck and jumped out, making her way over to Brianna who grabbed her in a fierce little hug. "Mom, Dad, this is my roommate, Madison. She's funny and smart and really, really good with plants. She can shoot and take care of animals and I can't wait until you meet her parents."

Brianna waved at Madison's mom and dad and they waved back. "Mrs. Sloane can make dinner out of a can of peas and thin air and her dad can fend off a billion men with a handgun and crappy flashlight. Oh!" She squealed as Peyton hopped out of the Jeep. "And Peyton! He can chop all the firewood!"

Everyone standing around in the little circle laughed. Brianna's mom wiped at her face and held out her hand to Madison. "Welcome to the Clifton cabin, Madison. It's a pleasure to have all of you."

Her father hobbled over to stand next to Madison and introduced himself. After everyone shook hands, he cleared his throat. "Brianna insisted that you would want us to stay, but I want to just say from the beginning that we don't have to. We know this is your land and your cabin and we are more than happy to find our own way."

Brianna's mother glanced at her father and smiled. "We couldn't be happier that you're here."

Fireball meowed and hopped out of the truck before scampering over and weaving through everyone's legs. Madison looked around at all the happy faces and wiped at her eyes. There would be hard work, hot days, and cold nights, but together, they would make it.

They would turn this apocalypse into a new beginning.

ACKNOWLEDGMENTS

Thank you for reading the beginning of the *After the EMP* saga. Although I hate to say goodbye to the Sloane family, new stories set in the same post-apocalyptic universe are coming!

Other characters are facing their own struggles in this new post-apocalyptic landscape and their stories are begging to be told. If you've read *Darkness Falls*, then you'll have an idea of just who I mean!

This series has been a joy and a struggle to write since the beginning and I couldn't have done it without amazing readers and a supportive family. Writing about ordinary families thrust into an uncertain future paints my everyday life with my own family in a whole new light.

I hope I've entertained you on this journey! I'll be back with all new *After the EMP* characters (and a few familiar faces) soon.

Until next time,
Harley

ALSO BY HARLEY TATE

Have you read Darkness Falls, the exclusive companion short story to the After the EMP series? If not you can get it for free by subscribing to my newsletter:

www.harleytate.com/subscribe

If you were hundreds of miles from home when the world ended, how would you protect your family?

Walter started his day like any other by boarding a commercial jet, ready to fly the first leg of his international journey. Halfway to Seattle, he witnesses the unthinkable: the total loss of power as far as he can see.

Hundreds of miles from home, he'll do whatever it takes to

get back to his wife and teenage daughter. Landing the plane is only the beginning.

Darkness Falls is a companion story to *After the EMP*, a post-apocalyptic thriller series following the Sloane family and their friends as they attempt to survive after a geomagnetic storm destroys the nation's power grid.

If you haven't checked out *Darkness Falls*, I hope you do so soon - you just might see a few familiar faces in book four of *After the EMP*!

ABOUT HARLEY TATE

When the world as we know it falls apart, how far will you go to survive?

Harley Tate writes edge-of-your-seat post-apocalyptic fiction exploring what happens when ordinary people are faced with impossible choices.

Harley's first series, *After the EMP*, follows the Sloane family and their friends as they try to survive in a world without power. When the nation's power grid is wrecked, it doesn't take long for society to fall apart. The end of life as we know it brings out the best and worst in all of us.

The apocalypse is only the beginning.

Contact Harley directly at:

www.harleytate.com
harley@harleytate.com

Made in United States
Troutdale, OR
08/18/2023